Mills & Boon
Best Seller Romance

A chance to read and collect some of the best-loved novels from Mills & Boon—the world's largest publisher of romantic fiction.

Every month, four titles by favourite Mills & Boon authors will be re-published in the *Best Seller Romance* series.

A list of other titles in the *Best Seller Romance* series can be found at the end of this book.

Rachel Lindsay

FORBIDDEN LOVE

MILLS & BOON LIMITED
LONDON · TORONTO

All the characters in this book have no existence outside the imagination of the Author, and have no relation whatsoever to anyone bearing the same name or names. They are not even distantly inspired by any individual known or unknown to the Author, and all the incidents are pure invention.

The text of this publication or any part thereof may not be reproduced or transmitted in any form or by any means, electronic or mechanical, including photocopying, recording, storage in an information retrieval system, or otherwise, without the written permission of the publisher.

This book is sold subject to the condition that it shall not, by way of trade or otherwise, be lent, resold, hired out or otherwise circulated without the prior consent of the publisher in any form of binding or cover other than that in which it is published and without a similar condition including this condition being imposed on the subsequent purchaser.

First published 1977
Australian copyright 1984
Philippine copyright 1984
This edition 1984

© Rachel Lindsay 1977

ISBN 0 263 74616 X

Set in Linotype Plantin 10 on 10½ pt.
02-0384

Made and printed in Great Britain by Richard Clay (The Chaucer Press) Ltd, Bungay, Suffolk

'I'm glad to hear it. From the way Sir William described you, I wasn't sure you would.'

'What did he say?' she asked curiously.

'He described you as being the soul of tact and discretion.'

Venetia gave a rueful smile. 'It makes me sound frightfully predictable and dull!'

'At the moment it's an attribute I tend to value.'

The words seemed wrested from him, and though she longed to know what he meant, she pretended not to see anything odd in his remark, nor to notice the sudden restlessness with which he moved from the mantelpiece to the desk, and then back again.

'You *are* tactful,' he said suddenly. 'You're overwhelmed with curiosity, yet you're sitting there like a—like a——'

'Mouse,' she ventured, keeping her voice light.

'An eminently sensible young mouse!'

For the first time since meeting him she warmed to him, but she kept her expression as blank as his. She had come here as secretary to his wife and she must remember that this was her only function.

'I assume you are aware that I personally asked Sir William to find a companion for my wife,' Neil Adams went on as though divining her thoughts.

'He said a social secretary was required. He omitted to mention the word "companion".'

'Perhaps he thought that would follow naturally if you and Margot liked one another. My wife finds it extremely dull here. That's why it's so important that she—that she has someone with her whom she likes.'

'I'll do my best, Mr Adams, though I'm not sure what we have in common.'

'You're both young and you're both English.'

'That applies to a lot of other women out here!'

'Margot finds them too colonial. But I rather suspect she means provincial.' One long, thin finger touched his chin. 'You may find her somewhat highly-strung. She's had a great deal of personal tragedy and this has—has affected her.'

'You don't need to apologise for Mrs Adams' moods.' Venetia decided to be blunt, knowing she might not get the opportunity again. 'I wasn't sent out here to be mollycoddled. I came so that it would be possible for *you* to remain here for the next six months. The trade talks are important. If they weren't, I wouldn't have agreed to do as Sir William asked.'

There was a sharp silence, finally broken by the man giving a dry smile. 'You're nothing if not forthright, Miss Jackson.'

'I think it's best in the circumstances. But I don't mean to be rude.'

'You weren't. However, I still think you should be aware of some of the details. It will make your stay here less difficult. As I was saying a moment ago, my wife has suffered considerable personal tragedy. Her twin brother, to whom she was deeply attached, was killed four years ago in a skiing accident. We were on our way to his funeral when we were involved in an accident too. It had an equally tragic outcome for us, and the—the two circumstances, coming together the way they did, were more than she could cope with emotionally.' There was a pause. 'She has never managed to regain her equilibrium.'

Venetia wondered why he spoke in such old-fashioned terminology. If he were trying to say that the two accidents had caused his wife to have a nervous breakdown—from which she was still undoubtedly suffering—he was going about it in an awfully long-winded way. But perhaps a man of his type—reserved to the point of withdrawal—found it difficult to unburden himself to anyone.

'You don't need to make any excuses for your wife's behaviour, Mr Adams,' she said quietly. 'I realise she can be difficult, but as I've already told you, I came here for a purpose and I will remain until that purpose has been accomplished.'

His look was keen, but she faced it with candour, and it was his eyes that wavered first.

'My wife has no idea that you came here under orders,' he said.

'She won't learn of it from me.'

'Good. I would also appreciate it if you did not mention what I have told you about her.'

'I'm the soul of discretion,' Venetia reminded him.

'Then you'll be the first woman who is!'

The joke was unexpected and she took a moment to react to it. By the time she did, he was opening the door of a black and gold lacquer cabinet.

'Would you like a drink, Miss Jackson?'

'I'd love one.'

'There's nothing alcoholic, I'm afraid. Only fruit juice and tomato juice.'

She hid her surprise. 'Tomato juice, then.'

'I can pep it up with Worcester sauce if you like,' he said gravely.

'I'll have it straight,' she said, equally gravely, and watched as he brought her a frosted glass filled to the brim. She saw that he was drinking the same, and wondered whether it was religion or taste that made him teetotal.

'Don't you drink at all?' she asked.

'Sometimes.' He raised his glass. 'To your stay here, Miss Jackson. I hope it will be a pleasant one.'

Acknowledging the toast, she sipped her drink, musing on all she had just learned of Margot Adams. Her brother's death explained her high-strung tension and also her husband's surprising subservience to it, but what was the second tragedy to which he had referred? She had the impression he had meant more than a motor accident. Could Margot have been permanently injured by it? If so, it was not visible to the eye. She was still thinking about this when a gong rang out, and Neil Adams glanced at his watch.

'My wife doesn't appear to have heard it. Would you mind telling her that we are waiting for her?'

Venetia thought the gong was sufficiently loud to have been heard all over the house, but she forbore to say so, and sped up to the first floor. Only as she reached it did she realise she didn't know where Margot Adams' room was, and she was wondering what to do when an elderly Chinese manservant appeared. He directed her to a corner room on the opposite side of the house from her own, and she rapped on the panelled door. There was no sound and she rapped again.

'Mrs Adams!' she called. 'It's me—Venetia Jackson.'

A key turned in the lock and the door opened. Margot Adams looked at her, her magnolia skin unusually flushed.

'The gong has gone,' Venetia said. 'Your husband sent me to tell you.'

'To spy on me, you mean! Do you want to come in and snoop around?'

'What for?' Venetia asked, puzzled.

Margot stared at her, then the smooth lids came down to hide the blue eyes. 'Just my silly joke,' she said, and closing the door behind her, linked her hand in a friendly fashion with Venetia's. It was a dry and bony hand, with a faint tremble in it that indicated tension. 'Perhaps you'll be able to improve the food while you're here. Our cook insists on serving Chinese meals. I swear to heaven I'll turn into a rice ball one day!'

Venetia laughed. 'You don't look the type to be intimidated by your cook, Mrs Adams.'

'I only put up a fight for things I care about—and I can't get worked up over food. Incidentally, I asked you to call me Margot.'

Venetia bit her lip, wondering why she should find it so hard to comply. There was only a few years' difference in age between herself and Mrs Adams, and certainly no difference in class or culture. Yet she could not think of the woman as anything other than by her married name.

'Never mind,' Margot said gaily. 'You'll get used to my name in time. You're obviously one of the old school—like Neil. He's stuffy too!'

'I'm sure he isn't,' Venetia protested.

'I know my husband better than you.' Margot was annoyed. 'He's stuffed so full of protocol that there's no room for feelings!'

Neil Adams was already in the dining room when they entered it, standing by the centre of the beautifully laid table. Margot motioned Venetia to sit beside her so that they both faced him, and then asked with amusement if he felt like a mandarin supping with his two concubines.

He took the teasing in good part, and though Venetia would not have gone so far as to say he unbent, he did seem to be more relaxed, as though he had expected a blow to fall which had been avoided. Had he been anticipating another row with his wife? she wondered, and devoutly hoped she would not be present when it happened.

'The cook's really done us proud tonight.' Margot's quick voice broke into Venetia's thoughts. 'It must be in honour of your arrival. It's the first time he's served lamb chops in one piece. Usually he cuts them into bits and smothers them with soy sauce!'

'My wife doesn't appreciate Chinese cooking,' her husband explained. 'Do you like it, Miss Jackson?'

'I'm afraid I only know the chop-suey variety. I don't think I've ever had authentic Chinese food.'

'Well, you'll wallow in it here,' Margot said. 'Unless you're willing to take Lee Hok in hand. He *can* cook English food—if he deigns to.'

'I don't think coping with Lee Hok is part of Miss Jackson's duties,' Neil Adams remarked.

'Venetia's already promised to talk to him.'

With a forkful of food halfway to her mouth, Venetia quickly inserted it and began to chew. Suspecting her silence, Neil Adams gave her a sharp look, although he made no comment, but it warned her to be careful of him: he might say little, but he obviously saw much.

She glanced at Margot. The room was lit by candles and it softened the girl's features and made her look ethereally beautiful. It had the opposite effect on the man, for the gentle light robbed his hair of colour, making it appear silver and giving him an ascetic look that went well with his pale, glittering eyes and thin, tight-set mouth. She saw his hand come up to his face and knew it to be a nervous gesture of which he was unaware. It made her notice his cheek, and she saw it was more rounded than she had expected, with a delicate curve that made it look curiously vulnerable.

'You've forgotten the wine.' Margot's voice broke the silence. 'I know *I* don't drink, but I'm sure Venetia does.'

Only then did Venetia notice the absence of wine glasses. 'If neither of you drink,' she said hastily, 'please don't bother about me.'

'But Neil adores wine,' his wife replied. 'He's only stopped drinking it because of me. I'm teetotal. I keep telling him I don't mind if he drinks, but he doesn't believe me.'

'Some people don't enjoy drinking alone,' Venetia said tactfully.

'But he won't be drinking alone—not now *you're* here!' Margot waved a thin arm. 'Open a bottle, Neil. I'd do it myself if I had the key.' She gave a wide smile in Venetia's direction. 'Neil guards the wine cellar as if it's a cave of gold.'

'I have some excellent vintages,' he said quietly, and then to Venetia: 'It's difficult to have a good cellar out here unless you know a year in advance that you're coming. Then it gives you time to ship out the wine and let it settle.'

'You see what a connoisseur he is,' Margot said admiringly, her red-gold hair glowing like fire in the light, as she nodded her head with every word. 'Everything has to be perfect, even down to no sediment in the bottle!' She pushed back her chair. 'Give me the keys, Neil, and I'll bring you a bottle.'

'Lo can get it.'

'Isn't it late to bother now?' Venetia said quickly. 'We've

nearly finished dinner and the wine will be too cold anyway.'

'Don't tell me *you're* a knowledgeable imbiber too?' Margot exclaimed.

'It isn't very knowledgeable to know about wine temperatures.'

Margot gave a shrug. 'Open a bottle of white, then—or champagne.' She clapped her hands. 'Yes, have some champagne—that goes with everything.'

Neil Adams turned to the middle-aged servant standing in the shadows at the end of the dining room. 'A bottle of champagne, Lo. The Bollinger.'

Within a couple of moments champagne was fizzing into tall, fluted glasses.

'Not for me,' said Margot, shaking her head as the butler went to fill her glass.

'Have you always been teetotal?' Venetia asked.

'For the last few years. Though being out here is enough to drive anyone to drink!'

'It's only for another six months,' Neil Adams said. 'Possibly even less.'

'Six days are too long!' Margot retorted, and swung round to Venetia. 'How would you like to be stuck in a hole like this when you had a marvellous home in England?'

'I don't think Miss Jackson wants to be involved in our quarrels,' her husband said.

'She'll have to be if she's going to stay here! Everyone knows I hate this place. If you had any feelings for me you'd have packed up and left ages ago. You wouldn't even have come here in the first place!'

'I couldn't refuse. You know that.'

'Because the Prime Minister asked you! The Government wouldn't have collapsed if you'd said no!'

'Margot, *please*,' Neil Adams pleaded.

'*Please*,' his wife mocked. 'Why don't you try and please *me*? After all, you *are* my husband. You'll never be father to my children, but you're *still* my husband!'

'For God's sake!' he burst out.

'For *my* sake!' Margot cried, and jumping to her feet, ran from the room.

Slowly the man stood up and followed her, pausing momentarily by the door. 'Forgive me, Miss Jackson, I——' Abruptly he walked out.

The depression Venetia had felt earlier that evening was nothing to the depression she felt now, as she sat alone at the huge table in the candlelit dining room, empty save for herself and a dim figure by the sideboard. Her appetite had long since gone, shrivelled up by the intensity of Margot Adams' anger. If tonight was a foretaste of meals to come, she was in for a very slimming time. Unless of course she became used to scenes the way Neil Adams had obviously done, for here he was again, resuming his seat and his meal as though nothing had happened. She glanced at him from beneath her lashes. Not quite as if nothing had happened, she amended, for there was a fine but perceptible shine of perspiration on his upper lip.

'You mustn't let my wife's scenes worry you,' he said quietly. 'She doesn't mean half the things she says.'

Venetia nodded without replying. Was he so blind where his wife was concerned that he couldn't see how badly she was behaving, or was he a weakling in his private life? Yet she had not thought him to be weak when they had first met. She sighed. Perhaps she was not such a good judge of character after all.

CHAPTER FOUR

WITHIN a week Venetia felt she had known Margot Adams a lifetime, and a lifetime fraught with difficulties, she thought as, for the third time in one morning, she was asked to re-type the arrangements for a forthcoming charity luncheon to be held at the Peninsula Hotel the following month.

Working in the Press department of the Foreign Office she had dealt with many different employers, and had learned to accept the vagaries of them all, but she had found none as difficult or changeable as the beautiful, spoiled woman whose whims she had promised to obey for the next six months.

Considering Margot's intelligence, her behaviour was inexplicable, for she seemed to take delight in stretching people to the limit of their endurance, almost as if she were testing how far she could go with them. Not only did she do this with Venetia, but with her husband too, though so far Venetia had not seen him lose his temper. Indeed the more obstreperous Margot became, the more placatory he was in return, until eventually the aggression she directed towards him turned upon itself, and she would dissolve into tears and apologies. As always, this elicited an immediate response from him, and Venetia would hurry from the room to avoid seeing him take Margot in his arms.

Her initial irritation with what she regarded as his subservient attitude had hardened into something stronger, and she marvelled that he could deal astutely with other men yet be so foolish with his wife. Could he have married her for her money and the prestige of her family? Was that why he gave in to her? As Sir William had said, the Destrys were well known in political life, and if he was a member of that family Neil's talents would not be overlooked. She wondered what his own background was, and made a note to try and find out. The library in the British Embassy might have a *Who's Who* that would tell her.

She was unwilling to make a special journey to town to look at it, so her curiosity remained unsatisfied until the beginning of the following week, when Margot, dictating a letter to a cousin who lived in Devon, mentioned that this was where she had first met Neil.

'He was Cynthia's beau, actually,' she explained. 'They were neighbours and they grew up together. But he was always away when I went to stay with Cynthia—first at Eton and then at Oxford—so I never met him until I was twenty-four.' She saw Venetia's eyes widen. 'Yes, I'm thirty-five,' she said gaily, 'but I don't look it, do I?'

'I thought you were only a few years older than me,' Venetia admitted.

'The Destrys have always looked younger than their years. It can't be from pious living, so it must be good bone structure!'

They were in Margot's bedroom and as she spoke she wandered over to a bureau and from the bottom drawer took out an album. She opened one of the pages and dropped the book on to Venetia's lap. 'That's what Neil and I were like when we met.'

Venetia stared at the photographs. Margot looked exactly as she did today, a little less brittle perhaps, but with the same wild beauty. It was the man who was entirely different; lean, yet not as thin as he was now, with a carefree expression that had since been totally lost. It was not so much that his outward appearance had changed, but that his inner one had altered; as if years of coping with a capricious wife had robbed him of spirit and vitality.

Margot flicked the page to a lovely grey stone manor house. 'That's Neil's home. He'd like to live there permanently, but I can't stand it for more than a week at a time.'

'Are Mr Adams' parents alive?' Venetia asked curiously.

'Only his mother. She never wanted him to go into

politics, but he was so brilliant at Oxford that it was a foregone conclusion.' She gave a slight smile. 'He's always had things the easy way. A double first without any swotting; a rugger blue—you name it, he had it. Even meeting me was an act of good fortune. With *his* ability and Destry influence he couldn't fail to get to the top.'

'I'm sure he didn't marry you for those reasons.'

'I don't need *you* to tell me that!' Margot flashed.

'I'm sorry,' Venetia said hurriedly. 'I didn't mean to——'

'I know you didn't.' The woman's good humour was restored. 'Neil was madly in love with me. That's why he married me. And he'd have married me if I'd been a Destry or a dustman's daughter!'

'It must be wonderful to be loved in that way,' said Venetia.

'Haven't *you* been?'

'Not since I was thirteen. And then he was most unsuitable. Three years younger than me and fat!'

'I don't believe a word of it!' Margot laughed. 'You must have masses of suitors.'

'Not even one.' Unwilling for the catechism to continue, Venetia closed the photo album and stood up. 'I've a lot of letters to type for you. I'd better get started or I'll miss the post.'

'Blow the post!' Margot was suddenly petulant. 'Stay and talk to me. I don't want to be alone.'

Recognising this as yet another change of mood, Venetia bit back a sigh. The more she came to know Margot, the more convinced she was that the woman was unstable. Too much money and not enough to do, she thought with asperity, and ignoring the order she had been given, picked up her portable typewriter and went to the door.

'You're to stay here and keep me company,' Margot commanded. 'If you don't, I'll fire you!'

'I'll be perfectly happy to go.'

Margot's reply was a foul epithet that made Venetia's face flame. 'I'd appreciate you not swearing at me, Mrs Adams,' she said angrily. 'That's one thing I won't tolerate.'

'*You* won't tolerate?' Margot burst out laughing. 'My dear girl, you've no choice in the matter!'

Clamping her lips tight, Venetia flung open the door and moved forward blindly, not seeing the tall spare figure until she collided with it and her typewriter went crashing to the ground.

'If you break that machine you'll pay for it,' Margot shrilled.

Venetia bent to pick it up, but was prevented from doing so by the grip of lean, hard hands.

'Allow me,' Neil Adams said in an expressionless voice, and bent to retrieve the typewriter.

Venetia took it from him, but as she went to move away he stepped in front of her, his eyes going from her flushed face to Margot's pale one.

'It looks as though I've arrived just in time.'

'You certainly have!' his wife said furiously. 'Venetia seems to have forgotten why she was brought here. You'd better remind her that she's supposed to keep me company —not go and stick herself in the library all the time!'

'I have a whole notebook of letters to type,' Venetia said evenly, 'and I was told they were urgent.'

'So what's the problem?' the man asked quietly. 'If my wife has changed her mind about the importance of the letters, surely——'

'It was a little more than that,' Venetia interrupted. 'I'll accept temper and capriciousness, Mr Adams, but I refuse to be sworn at.' Only then did she see that she had got under his skin, for it suffused with colour. The pinkness made him look unexpectedly young, reminding her vividly of the photograph she had seen in the album.

'Sworn at?' he repeated.

'I lost my temper,' Margot said. She was standing close to them and she twined herself against her husband's body, her scarlet nails resting on his jacket. 'For goodness sake, Neil, tell Venetia not to be so prissy!'

'*You* could try being a little less robust,' he said jocularly.

'You know what I'm like when I get angry. I suddenly start remembering things and then I lose control.' The blue eyes were like limpid pools. 'I don't mean to be rude, Neil, you know that, don't you?'

'I know,' he said soothingly, and glanced at Venetia, faint warning in his eyes. 'If Margot wants you to stay and talk to her, I think you can overlook your shorthand notebook!' He clasped his arm firmly on the typewriter. 'I'll take this down and leave it in the library.'

'I don't need Venetia now you're here,' Margot said. 'She can get on with the letters as long as *you'll* stay with me.'

'I have some papers to go over.'

'Do it here.'

'But I——'

'You're not to leave me alone,' Margot cried, and spun back into her room. 'Come here, Neil!' she ordered.

Flinging Venetia another look, he obeyed the summons.

Slowly Venetia went down to the library. As always when she witnessed a scene between Neil Adams and his wife, she was astonished at his docility, more so because it did not fit in with the firmness of character he must possess to have carved such a brilliant career for himself. Opening her notebook, she began to type, but her thoughts were still with the couple upstairs, and she found herself making so many mistakes that she eventually stopped typing and decided to go for a stroll in the garden.

She was halfway across the hall when the telephone rang. It was picked up almost at once and she hesitated, wondering if there was a message she would be expected to take, but when Lo came out it was to tell her that the call was for her. Surprised, she hurried to the receiver, and hearing Simon Hoy's friendly voice, found it in such direct contrast to her own nervous irritation that she greeted him more warmly than she might otherwise have done.

'I hope you've had a chance to settle down,' he said, 'and that you're free to have lunch with me tomorrow.'

She hesitated. She had not yet arranged the hours she

would be working, but as she had not had any free time since her arrival, she did not see a problem in going out for a few hours tomorrow. 'I'm sure I can get away,' she replied. 'Where shall we meet?'

'I'll collect you.'

Remembering Neil Adams' frigid remarks about Simon, she decided it would be wiser if he didn't.

'I have to go into Victoria in the morning,' she lied, 'so it will be easier if I meet you there.'

'Fine. The Mandarin at twelve-thirty. In the reception hall.'

She replaced the receiver in a far lighter mood than the one in which she had picked it up. It would do her good to get out of the house and see other faces. Staying in this difficult emotional atmosphere was making her edgy.

But when she went down to dinner later that evening she had no chance to tell Margot, for only Neil Adams appeared in the dining room.

'Margot has a migraine,' he explained. 'She's gone to bed.'

'There are some excellent pills one can take for it,' she said, 'but you have to take them the moment you feel the symptoms.'

'I know.' His voice was cool. 'Unfortunately I wasn't with Margot the whole time. I had to leave her for a while and when I—when I saw her again it was too late.'

'Would you like me to go and sit with her?'

'No,' he said quickly. 'When she isn't well she prefers to be left alone.' He sat down at the table and immediately the first course was served.

As always the food was Chinese, and Venetia noticed that he only toyed with it, pushing the little pieces of meat from one side of the plate to the other, and barely eating more than a small portion.

'No wonder you're so thin,' she exclaimed, and then stopped, aghast at her effrontery. But he did not seem to mind and merely gave a non-committal shrug. Gaining confidence from his silence, she said: 'Would you like to have a steak?'

'No, thank you.' He hesitated. 'I doubt if we have any, anyway.'

'I'm sure there are steaks in the kitchen,' she pressed, and picked up a piece of meat with her fork. 'I bet you a million this is fillet.'

'You'd never know it,' he said, with the first sign of irritability she had seen from him. 'By the time they cut it, soak it and fry it, one's hard put to know *what* it is!'

'I'll get you something else.' Before he could stop her she hurried out.

She had been to the kitchen several times, first to make the acquaintance of the cook—which she had decided was the right thing to do if she were going to stay here for any length of time—and again to watch the preparation of Peking Duck, an elaborate recipe that took many hours to prepare. Now she found that her earlier show of friendliness stood her in good stead, for her request for a steak brought forth a succulent-looking T-bone, and she darted forward just in time to stop the cook from beating it flat with a mallet. Hesitantly she asked if she could prepare it herself, and was relieved when the man beamed and bowed her towards a sizzling grill.

A quarter of an hour later she carried a tray to the dining room; on it was a crisp green salad glistening with vinaigrette dressing, a tender steak and some plain boiled potatoes which she had seen simmering in a pot preparatory to being used in a dumpling mixture.

Trying to keep her face expressionless, she set the tray in front of Neil Adams, but she could not help smiling as she saw the eager way he speared a potato and ate it. Sitting down again, she resumed her own meal. It was the first time they had dined alone together, in fact the first time she had been alone with him since the night of her arrival.

'That's the best meal I've had in months,' he said at last, putting his knife and fork down on an empty plate.

'Don't you have European food when you're out?'

'Frequently, but it's not the same as home cooking. You did it, didn't you?' At her nod he added: 'It was excellent. Just the way I like my meat. How did you know?'

'You're too fastidious to eat it rare, yet not such a Philistine to have it burned to a cinder!'

His chuckle—unexpectedly warm by comparison with his voice, which was cool—came across the table, and she realised she had never heard him laugh before.

'*You* should have been the diplomat, Miss Jackson, not me!'

'We both need to be,' she said, and then stopped, embarrassed as she realised how her words could be misconstrued.

Indeed his reaction showed all too clearly that he had taken them as reference to the scene earlier that evening, for he frowned and ran his hand over his hair, ruffling its smooth surface so that the pale strands stood up and caught the light, looking even more silvery fair than usual.

'I warned you Margot could be—can be emotional. You mustn't let yourself be upset by what she says. *I'm* not.'

'You're married to her.'

'For better or worse, you mean?'

She acknowledged his quickness and he gave a slight smile.

'Even usage hasn't made it easy for me to turn the other cheek, Miss Jackson. I have to keep reminding myself that Margot can't help it. It's part of her illness. As for her wanting you to stay with her and keep her company . . .' He hesitated. 'I'd like you to do so. She gets moments of intense depression when she can't bear to be alone. Having someone around is helpful.'

'I hadn't realized.' Venetia was contrite. 'I thought she was acting rather more spoiled than usual. I'm sorry, that sounds rude, but——'

'You're entitled to be blunt. It's pointless to pretend about your reason for being here. As you have already said, you came out to help *me*, not Margot.'

'*Am* I helping you?'

'My wife is still in Hong Kong,' he said drily. 'That's the crux of the matter.'

'How are your negotiations going with the Chinese?' She deliberately changed the subject.

'Two steps forward and one step back! But eventually it will all be concluded.'

'Isn't it difficult to deal with Orientals? They're so inscrutable.'

'Only on the surface. Their inscrutability stems from the belief that it's bad manners to show your feelings.' He sighed. 'You've no idea how much I appreciate their phlegmatic attitude and calmness.' His glance was unexpectedly rueful. 'Or perhaps you have?'

'Yes,' she murmured, thinking of the woman upstairs. 'I certainly have.'

Dinner over, Venetia went to retire to her room, but to her surprise he asked if she would like to listen to some records. She had not heard any music since her arrival in Hong Kong, and she was delighted at the offer.

'Do you have an particular choice?' he asked as they went into the library.

'Anything except Prokofiev.'

'Anything?'

'I've catholic tastes,' she said firmly. 'I like the classics, jazz and the blues.'

'Jazz and the blues you can keep!' he replied.

'I bet you like Bach and Handel!'

'I appreciate passionate music too,' he said perceptively, and she flushed, aware that she had been put in her place.

Soon the strains of a cantata seeped into the room and gradually she felt herself unwind. She closed her eyes and relaxed, not moving as the Bach was replaced by a Mozart horn concerto and this in turn by Beethoven's Sonata Pathétique, which brought a lump to her throat and made her intensely aware of the man sitting opposite her. How cool and detached he was; almost as if it was only his physical body that was present, and his spirit had gone somewhere far away.

Knowing he was unaware of her, she was able to study him, and she looked at the soft fair hair lying like a cap of satin on his head. It was a well-shaped head, she noticed, and he had a well-shaped profile to go with it: a high forehead, an arched, uncompromising nose, and a wide, thin mouth. No, not thin, she amended, staring at it, but finely shaped, with a delicate curve to the upper lip and a slight fullness to the lower one which he disguised by the tight manner in which he held it, almost as if he were afraid of giving himself away. His paleness was deceptive too, for looking closely at him one saw imperceptible colour: a faint flush on his high cheekbones, pinkness at his temples and blue shadows on the masking lids that so frequently hid his unusually light brown eyes. But the eyes were not hidden at the moment; they were open wide and staring into space, affording her a full view of them.

No wonder he kept them hidden, she thought with an unexpected pang, for there was so much sadness in them that she felt she was seeing into the depths of his soul. How large and clear the irises were, and how deep and dark the pupils, wide now because of the half-light. No man had the right to look so vulnerable. It gave him an advantage over other people. She dismissed the thought at once. Neil Adams never used his advantage. Indeed, he masked his feelings beneath a layer of frigid detachment. Margot was cruel to provoke him the way she did. He must love her deeply if he could stand her unreasonable moods.

He stirred in his chair and she averted her gaze, but she was not quick enough and their eyes met. At once his lids half closed, turning his eyes into glittering slits that seemed to bore into her, stripping away her veneer and exposing her thoughts. Ashamed that she had been caught out, and trembling with an emotion she could not analyse, she resolutely looked at the carpet. She must not allow herself to be so touched by this man. It was stupid to confuse vulnerability with weakness, and she would do well to remember that Neil Adams *was* weak.

The music came to an end and he uncrossed his legs, speaking in a voice far huskier than she had heard before. 'I rarely let myself play the Pathétique. It moves me too much.'

'Don't you like being moved?'

'Not any more. I find it more civilised not to probe one's emotions.' He stood up and switched off the record-player. 'A nightcap, Miss Jackson?'

Knowing herself dismissed, she shook her head and bade him goodnight. 'Thank you for letting me hear your records. I enjoyed them.'

'Play them yourself any time you wish,' he replied.

Alone in her room she mused over their conversation, wondering why he deliberately excluded emotion from his life. Was it because he felt so deeply that he no longer wanted to feel at all, or had his beautiful and wayward wife already taken so much out of him that he had no emotion left for anything else? Either way it showed him to be a man living on the surface of his potential, and she felt inexplicably sad, as though much of value was being left untouched.

CHAPTER FIVE

VENETIA did not see Margot before she left the house the next morning, for there was a note on her breakfast tray from Neil Adams telling her his wife was still unwell and did not wish to be disturbed.

Though she was reluctant to go out without obtaining permission—she wished she had had the foresight to have mentioned it to Neil Adams last night—there was nothing she could do about it now, and she set off to catch the funicular that would take her down to Victoria. It was strange how rarely she had heard it called by that name, for the word 'Hong Kong' was used far more frequently, and seemed to refer not only to the island but also the main city on it. She really must start to explore her surroundings. Not just Hong Kong island itself, but the peninsula of Kowloon and the New Territory behind it: four hundred square miles of mountains, valleys and inlets that served to provide the four million people of the Colony with a large part of their food. But it was the land beyond the New Territory—China itself—which inspired her imagination, and she wondered wistfully if there was any chance of her being able to go there. She was sure Neil Adams could arrange it, but knew a strong reluctance to ask any favours of him, in the same way that she did not want to take advantage of the car and chauffeur he normally left at his wife's disposal.

It was parked in the driveway as she left the house, and seeing her set off towards the front gate the driver came after her. When he learned she was going to catch the Peak Tram he insisted on taking her to the station, stating that it was too far for her to walk and informing her that she had already missed one of the small yellow mini-buses—halfway between a taxi and a bus—which travelled at frequent intervals at set routes around the Peak. Deciding it was easier to give in than to argue, Venetia allowed him to take her to the tram, flatly refusing his offer to drive her all the way down.

Several people were already waiting for the cable car, but she was lucky enough to find a seat at the front. However, she did not have much of a view because the steep angle of descent made it necessary for all the seats to face upwards, and in order to see the harbour she was forced to keep craning her neck round. At times she felt the cable car to be almost vertical, and she wondered, with a tingle of her scalp, what would happen if one of the cables snapped. A glance at the unconcerned Chinese and Europeans chattering around her told her she was being childish, and she stared determinedly through the windows until they reached the terminus.

Here she caught a tram and for twenty cents was swiftly transported along the steep roads to the business section. Consulting her tourist map, she got off at Chater Road, and almost immediately saw the back entrance of the Mandarin Hotel. She debated whether or not to go round to the front of the building, but a sharp wind blowing in from the sea was seeping through the lightweight wool of her orange suit, and decided her to take the entrance facing her.

An arcade of shops led to an escalator, which in turn took her to the first floor and another vast shopping area. Wishing she had more time to spare to look at the wonderful embroidered and beaded clothes and magnificent Chinese treasures—porcelain, ivories, gold carvings—she hurried to find her way to the Reception Hall where she was meeting Simon Hoy.

Not until she had walked three times round the shopping complex did she wearily decide it was easier to get out of Hampton Court maze than these winding intersections. Even the elevator she had entered had not gone down to the ground floor, but had whisked her instead to the top of the building, necessitating her descent in another lift which, once again, deposited her on the mezzanine floor.

There was only one thing to do and she did it. Returning to the street, she darted down a side turning and ran along the outside length of the hotel until she reached the main entrance. Sparing only a glance at the magnificently dressed porter, who looked like a cross between a mandarin and an Indian prince, she rushed into the reception hall.

Simon Hoy saw her at once. 'I thought you'd changed your mind about coming.'

'I got lost in the shopping arcade,' she explained.

He grinned. 'Where are all the parcels?'

'I wasn't buying—and I didn't have much time for looking either! I just thought it would be a short cut.'

'It is, if you know the way. But don't worry about being late. I'd have waited for you no matter what time you arrived.'

He propelled her past the long, busy reception desk to where a row of elevators were briskly disgorging and taking on passengers. As they waited for the one Simon wanted Venetia had her first clear glimpse of the hotel itself, and was disappointed to find the floor uncarpeted, though beautifully tiled, and a general air of noise and bustle she would have associated more with a busy provincial hotel than an elegant national one.

'Is it always so hectic here?' she asked, as a crowd of small Japanese men, all sporting cameras, poured past them.

'You're in the height of the tourist season,' Simon Hoy explained. 'From Christmas until the beginning of May it's always like this.'

Gilt doors slid open and he guided her into the elevator. Within seconds they emerged on to the top floor. Here was the peace and quiet she had found wanting downstairs, and feet sinking into thick-piled carpets, she was ushered by a Chinese waiter into a glass-walled bar that afforded a magnificent view of the harbour and one side of the city. Had it not been for the view, the bar could have been set in any major city of the world, and anxious to feast her eyes on it, she sat facing the window, hardly aware of what drink she had asked for until a Pimms was set in front of her.

'I'll arrange for you to lunch here tomorrow by yourself,' her escort said. 'Then you needn't bother talking to anyone!'

Scarlet-faced, she turned and looked at him, apologising for her rudeness.

'I thought you were looking forward to seeing *me*,' he said, only half placated.

'I am, but this is the first time I've been out since I arrived.'

He did not hide his surprise. 'But you've been here a week!'

'I didn't ask for time off,' she shrugged.

'It should have been given to you.'

'I can go out whenever I like.'

'I'll hold you to that,' he said. 'I would have rung you earlier except that my father was ill.'

She looked suitably sympathetic as he went into some detail about his father's illness. One rarely heard an Englishman talking so long on such a subject, and she remembered how family-conscious the Chinese were; like most of the Far East nations.

It was only in the northern climes, where colder weather gave cooler emotions, that the family unit had weakened. Venetia knew one would rarely see an old Chinese or Indian living alone so long as there was a younger relative who could be called on to provide a home for them. Such acceptance of duty to the aged had disadvantages for the young, she decided, but considerable advantages for the old.

'Haven't you ever wanted to live by yourself?' she asked.

'I do on occasion. We have a small flat in the city, and during the summer, if I'm caught by a typhoon, I use it. But the house is so beautiful that I prefer to live there.' His black, almond-shaped eyes, looked at her unwaveringly. 'You have promised to come and visit it, Venetia. You must let me know when you are free.'

Not sure if he meant for the day or weekend, she changed

the subject, only half listening as, in answer to her question, he told her a little about the history of Hong Kong.

In a faultlessly tailored grey suit Simon Hoy looked more westernised than she had recollected, though perhaps this was because her eyes had already grown used to sallow-skinned Chinese, with their small features and carbon-black hair.

Whatever the reason, she felt him to be less foreign, and was suddenly glad she had accepted his invitation to lunch. Remaining with Margot Adams in the luxurious yet stultified atmosphere of the house on the Peak, she had not realised how claustrophobic it had become until now, when she had shaken herself free of it.

A little later, in the restaurant, she felt another surge of pleasure as she sat facing him across the unusually large table which gave them yet another view of the glittering waters of Victoria harbour, and the masts and funnels of the boats anchored along the shore. The red and black décor of the room was Chinese, but the food was European and excellent, and Simon found his way round the menu with an ease that showed his familiarity with Western eating.

'We don't only have fried rice and noodles,' he teased, reading her thoughts.

'Was I as obvious as all that?'

'Only to me. But then I can always tell what you're thinking.'

'I'd better start to monitor my thoughts. No girl likes to have her secrets discovered!'

'Do you have many secrets, Venetia?' he asked.

'I thought you said you knew me.'

'Perhaps I should have said I'd like to know you better!' His voice was still teasing, although there was no humour in his expression nor the way in which his hand reached out across the table for hers.

She made a pretence of picking up her glass, though it was a gesture he saw through at once, since the glass was empty.

'When I saw you on the aircraft,' he said, 'you looked so composed I would never have guessed you were shy. Yet here you are avoiding my eyes and blushing like a schoolgirl.'

'I'm not blushing.' She faced him squarely. 'It's just that I find emotion embarrassing.'

'Are you scared of it?'

'I can see what it can do to a person,' she said involuntarily.

'So it's true what they say about the Adams,' Simon said.

She looked at him in silence, and he returned the look steadily, his narrow black brows drawn together.

'Who's "they"?' she asked lightly. 'And what do *they* say?'

'That Neil Adams is crazily in love with his wife and she can't see him for dirt!'

Venetia recoiled from the crudeness of the words, even though she could not deny the truth of them. But she had no intention of saying so. No matter how rife the gossip, she had no intention of adding to it.

'There must be some truth in it,' Simon Hoy continued. 'There's no smoke without fire.'

'I haven't seen any smoke for myself,' she said lightly. 'Anyway, why is everyone so interested in Mr and Mrs Adams?'

'Because of what he's trying to do and his position here. If his talks are successful, Hong Kong will face a boom period. Millions of pounds will go through it, both into and out of China.'

'And your business will virtually come to an end,' she said, deciding that the best way of changing the subject was to focus on his own affairs.

'You must have got *that* information from Adams.'

For the first time the young Chinese looked angry. Always before there had been a smile on his face and a quirk of amusement on his mouth. But now his eyes were slits and the soft timbre of his voice had gone high.

'Our business will have to change,' he admitted, 'but we

have no fear about making the transition satisfactorily. Instead of exporting *objets d'art* we will fill the boats with factory-made copies. The one priceless T'ang horse selling for thousands of pounds will be replaced by thousands of ceramic copies selling for as many pennies!'

'Won't you hate that?'

'Successful commerce has no time for sentiment. Naturally I love to handle beautiful objects, but then I have them in my own home, and if our business increases—as it will do if Mr Adams is successful—I will be able to afford even more!'

He spoke so positively that she was convinced he meant what he said, and made a mental note to tell Neil Adams. There must be many merchants in Simon's position, and if they felt the same way—and there was no reason why they shouldn't, for they were no less commercially-minded— then Neil Adams should get far less opposition than he was envisaging. Not that she could imagine opposition swaying him from any course upon which he had set himself. He was weak where his wife was concerned, but as far as outside factors went, she was certain he was implacable.

A waiter interrupted her thoughts by setting a grilled sole with a delicate champagne sauce in front of her, and she gave herself up to enjoyment of the meal. It was ridiculous to come away from the Adams' house and continue thinking about them; if she did that she might just as well not go out at all. Determinedly she gave her attention to her host and he responded happily. On the plane journey she had found him an amusing companion, but now she found him an interesting one too, with a good understanding of the Colony's affairs and a wide grasp of world problems, both trade and political.

'Unfortunately the two are frequently indivisible,' he said as she remarked on his knowledge. 'If one could obliterate politics from our daily life, there would be no problems regarding trade.'

'All the world a free port, you mean?'

He chuckled, a melodious, almost feminine sound. 'If

there were no trade restrictions, businesses like mine would be non-existent. A housewife could sit in her parlour in Wisconsin and read a Sears Roebuck mail-order catalogue compiled in Moscow or Peking!'

'You may get the Peking one even yet!'

'Only if Adams is successful, and there are many people who would like to see him fail.'

'Because it would affect their business?'

'I wasn't thinking so much in terms of money as of ideology. Several countries would be unhappy to see China involved with the West. Russia, for example, would prefer her to remain isolated, and so would Japan—though for different reasons.'

'I can see why the Russians and Chinese don't like each other,' Venetia said. 'China thinks the Russians should give them back the land the Czarists took from them, and the Russians think the opposite! But what are Japan's reasons?'

'Economic ones. Because of their vast labour force and high technical skill they can undercut everyone when it comes to costs. But the Chinese have an even greater labour force and no problems of unrest at all. Ally that to increasing technological knowledge—which is what Neil Adams will be promising them—and within ten years they'll be out-producing and undercutting the Japanese!'

She gave an exasperated sigh. 'How stupid of me not to know that for myself.'

'Why should you? Most women don't bother with trade and politics, and lovely ones like you should *never* do so.'

The emancipated woman in Venetia rose to the fore, but discretion forced her to swallow her annoyance. She had supposedly come to Hong Kong as Margot Adams' social secretary, and a girl who was willing to do that kind of work would not concern herself with world problems. If her godfather had not insisted she maintain secrecy about her background and capabilities she would have told Simon Hoy the truth about her position there and then.

'I'm not quite as dumb as I look,' she murmured. 'Even social secretaries have the vote!'

'Now I've made you cross,' he said swiftly, 'and all I meant was to flatter you. But if you want to learn about world affairs I'll be delighted to teach you.'

She closed her mind to her double first in Economics and Political Science. 'I don't think I'd be able to absorb it. I'll stick to being a secretary.'

'Have you ever thought of being a wife?'

The question caught her unawares. 'Of course. I'd love to get married and have children.'

'You'd need a husband first!'

'I wasn't thinking of an immaculate conception!' she laughed.

'Then do you have a particular man in mind?'

'No,' she said firmly, 'I haven't.'

'Perhaps you have met him already? I am sure it was fate that brought you to Hong Kong.'

'Not fate,' she disagreed. 'Mrs Adams.'

His banter vanished and he frowned. 'I still don't see you as a social secretary, I can't imagine you wanting to work for the lovely Margot—unless you had a special reason.'

'Perhaps I'm a Russian or Chinese spy.' She made herself chuckle, inwardly awarding him full marks for intuition. 'But is there a special type to be a social secretary?' she asked.

'There's only a special type who could stick your employer, and no girl of spunk and intelligence would.'

'Mrs Adams seems to have a formidable reputation here. I suppose it's because she's rich and beautiful. It always excites envy.'

'Even accounting for the envy of our middle-aged matrons,' he conceded, 'there's still no smoke without fire.'

'How banal can you get?' she said crossly.

'Is it banal to speak the truth?' His eyes went past her shoulder and came to rest on the other side of the room. 'The smoke and fire are coming in together.'

Forgetting the need for tact, Venetia swivelled round, her eyes at once seeing Margot's flaming hair. The migraine she had been suffering from had left no mark on the vivid face, with its full red mouth and eyes glowing like blue lamps. Having seen her only in diaphanous housecoats, Venetia saw with faint envy that even in an exquisitely tailored white suit she gave the impression of gliding. It was not so much the way she walked, which was grace in itself, but the air of buoyancy which emanated from her. All this and heaven too, Venetia thought wryly, and catching the thought before it went any further, wondered whether heaven mean money or a man. Not a man, she decided hastily. By no stretch of the imagination could one consider Neil Adams heaven-sent. A picture of him came into her mind: not as she always remembered him—pale, composed, austere—but as he had been last night when he had been listening to the Pathétique: his eyes tender and sad, his mouth relaxed so that the full lower lip had been disclosed.

Quickly she focused her attention on Margot's escort, and at once the words Beauty and the Beast came to mind. Simian, both as to hair and features, he was below average height, but so broad of shoulder that he dominated the room, exuding a virile strength that could be felt even at a distance. As he came closer she saw he was slim-hipped, with surprisingly small feet, and that he had a delicate, almost faun-like way of moving which gave no indication of his bulk. Like most of the men she had seen in the restaurant he was exceedingly well dressed. Either all the males in Hong Kong took great pride in their appearance, she thought, or it was impossible to find a bad tailor.

Hurriedly picking up a napkin, she half-covered her face as she turned back to Simon, hoping Margot Adams would go past without seeing her. But the blue eyes, darting around the room greeting and acknowledging greetings, spotted Venetia's jet black hair immediately she came abreast of it.

'So this is where you escaped to?' she teased, and turned with a smile to the man at her side. 'Boris darling, I'd like you to meet my new secretary and comfort, Venetia Jackson.'

Venetia acknowledged the introduction and felt her hand caught in an iron grip.

'Boris Kanin,' the man said in a voice that seemed to come from deep inside him. 'It is a pleasure to welcome such a beautiful import.'

'I told you she was lovely, didn't I?' Margot trilled. 'But you wouldn't believe me.'

'I never believe what anyone tells me,' came the calm answer. 'I need to see it with my own eyes.' Brown ones, with a reddish glint in them that gave them fire, raked Venetia from head to foot and, like fire, seemed to burn through her clothes.

Hurriedly she pulled her gaze away from him and looked at Margot. 'I'm sorry I didn't see you before leaving the house, but Mr Adams left me a note saying you didn't want to be disturbed.'

'That was silly of him. I was fine by this morning. And I've *told* you to call me Margot!' She swung round to her escort. 'English girls are so inhibited, Boris, and Venetia's worse than most.'

'I would have said better than most.' Again warm brown eyes rested on Venetia's face. 'Margot has no appreciation of convention. It is a trait one often finds in the lawless.'

'I wouldn't have called Mrs—my employer—lawless,' Venetia said coldly, irritated by the faint smile on Boris Kanin's swarthy face.

'Wait until you know her as well as I do.'

'No one will ever know me that well.' Margot's red-tipped hand rested on his sleeve. 'Come along, darling, we're interrupting a tête-à-tête.'

Only then did Venetia remember she had not introduced Simon and hurriedly she did so. The two men greeted each other with a marked lack of warmth though Margot gave one of her brilliant, all-embracing smiles and looked at him with eyes that did not see him, before she floated away to a window table some yards ahead. It was strange the way she could look at someone in such a blind way. Venetia had frequently seen her do it when her husband was speaking to her. It was as though she was reluctant to let her mind be held by someone else's, as if she were afraid of allowing another person to impinge on her senses. Yet with Boris Kanin she gave a totally different impression, and Venetia had the feeling that she was mentally clinging to him, if not physically too, she thought with a flicker of irritation as she saw the red-gold head bend over to look at the menu the man was holding, a necessary intimacy since she had dropped her own menu to the floor.

'You haven't answered me,' Simon complained, and Venetia realised that for the last few moments she had not heard a single word he had said. 'I obviously can't compete with a Russian,' he went on, as she apologised and asked him to repeat the question. 'Or were you deciding that I hadn't been gossiping after all?'

Her blank look told him she did not know what he meant. 'Boris Kanin,' he repeated, 'the fire and the smoke. You cannot deny *he* is the fire.'

'How can you be sure?'

'All Hong Kong knows they're having an affair. All Hong Kong except Neil Adams; or if he does know he's putting up an excellent front.'

Venetia was glad that at that moment a waiter came to take away their plates and set clean ones before them. Concentrating on the elaborate sweet trolley, she was given a breathing space before having to answer, and wondered whether she would need to answer at all if she pretended to concentrate long enough in choosing a sweet. Any doubts she might have had as to the truth of Simon's assertion had been dispelled by seeing Margot with Boris Kanin. No one could see them together and not know she was besotted over him. The word reverberated in her mind. Margot was as besotted over Boris as Neil Adams was besotted over her.

Pointing blindly at the trolley, she was surprised when a fluffy concoction of strawberry cream and meringue was set before her, and picking up a fork, she made a pretence of eating it. But the dismay pervading her affected her taste, and she might just as well have been eating sawdust.

'You seem to be taking the news very calmly,' Simon said, declining a sweet and ordering coffee.

'My employer's affairs are their own.'

'Only one affair for one employer,' he amended. 'No gossip besmirches the escutcheon of the Honourable Neil.'

'Why don't you like him?' she asked bluntly.

'Because he *is* so honourable!' Simon straightened his narrow shoulders. 'I don't like Boris Kanin either. Chinese aren't given to brawn, you know, and faced with Kanin . . .'

'Lots of women would feel the same,' she said quickly. 'He reminds me of a gorilla.' Simon's smile was instant, and she hid her own amusement. Who was it who had said that only women were receptive to flattery?

'I have kept the whole afternoon free,' he said. 'I thought you might like to drive around the city and take a quick trip over to Kowloon before we have dinner.'

'I hadn't planned on staying out the whole day.'

'It is your first day off in a week,' he reminded her.

'I'd still like to be home by tea-time.'

'I doubt if Mrs Adams will,' came the dry retort.

Looking at the couple ahead of her, deeply engrossed in each other, she knew it would be foolish to disagree.

'Even so, I'd like to get back,' she said. 'But I'll take you up on that drive round the city.'

As she walked from the restaurant she was aware of Boris Kanin looking at her and half raising his arm. It was a gesture almost mocking in its assurance and she ignored it and hurried out. It was always stimulating to know one had elicited desire in a man, yet in Boris's response to her there was something so animal and lustful that she felt degraded by it. How could Margot—with so ascetic a husband—be captivated by a man of such suffocating masculinity?

'Penny for your thoughts,' Simon said, giving her arm a little shake as they reached the elevator.

'You'd be wasting your money,' she smiled. 'They aren't worth that much.'

CHAPTER SIX

It was five o'clock and already dark when Simon Hoy drove Venetia back to the house.

'I'll be seeing you in a few days,' he murmured before he climbed back into his car. 'I intend becoming your official guide.'

'But not mentor!' she retorted, and heard him chuckle as she hurried into the house.

As he had foretold, Margot had not yet returned, and Venetia decided to shower and change before resuming her work, so that it was six-thirty when she finally seated herself at the typewriter in the library.

She was still typing when she heard a car in the drive, and peering through the window saw Margot emerge from it. Quickly she went back to the desk, and hardly had she seated herself when the woman came in. No one looking at her glazed eyes and flushed skin could doubt she had been well and truly loved. A feeling of sickness rose in Venetia and her fingers itched to slap the beautiful face and to take away the smile from the sensuous mouth.

'Been back long?' Margot asked, standing by the door and swaying slightly.

'An hour. I hope you didn't mind my going out?'

'Why should I? I was with Boris anyway, so there'd have been nothing for you to do.'

'I still have several letters to type, but I'll finish them this evening after dinner.'

'Another day won't matter,' Margot said, and swayed again.

'Aren't you feeling well?' Venetia half stood up but Margot backed away.

'I'm fine; just tired. I'll be all right when I've had a rest.'

She went across the hall, leaving Venetia to continue her

work. There was a strong smell of peppermint in the room and she made a face and forced herself to concentrate on her typing.

A sudden flood of light made her look up to see Neil Adams. He was wearing a dinner jacket and she realised it was later than she had imagined. With trembling hands she tidied the papers on the desk.

'I'm sorry, Mr Adams, I didn't realise the time.'

'There's no need to apologise for working late,' he smiled. 'I'm frequently guilty of it myself.' He came to stand by the mantelpiece. 'But there's no need for you to work such long hours, is there? I'll have a word with Margot and——'

'It has nothing to do with Mrs Adams,' Venetia interrupted. 'I went out to lunch and I got back late.'

'I see.' He clasped his hands behind his back. 'Did you go anywhere interesting?'

'I had lunch at the Mandarin Hotel and then went for a drive.'

'On a tour?'

'No, with Simon—Simon Hoy. The man I met on the plane coming over.'

'I remember,' he said without expression.

'I—we——' she stopped, wanting to talk to him yet surprised to find herself nervous. Putting the lid firmly on her typewriter, she began again. 'Your talks with the Chinese seem to be an open secret. Everyone apparently knows they're going on, and Simon says all the merchants here are terribly anxious for you to succeed.'

'I appreciate their hopes.'

'Aren't you pleased that people wish you well?'

He considered the question and said finally, 'Let us say that I don't mind if they don't.'

'How unfeeling you are!' She caught her breath. This was the second time she had let her tongue run away with her. If she did it again he would probably ask her to leave. Yet it would not be easy for him to do that. She had come here for a purpose, and until it had been completed, he needed her. Even so she owed him an apology. 'I'm sorry,

Mr Adams. I'm afraid that living on the job tends to breed familiarity. I won't let it happen again.'

'Don't make promises that I suspect you will be unable to keep!'

She saw he was smiling, and her nervousness dissolved. How friendly he could be when he wanted, though perhaps his normal coolness made even a slight thaw seem warmer than it was.

'What about a drink?' he suggested. 'Your usual tomato juice?'

'I'll be a devil and have pineapple!'

As he busied himself with the bottles she sat on her armchair, the soft folds of her red jersey dress falling around her.

'You remind me of a Christmas candle.' He was standing in front of her proffering a glass, and she took it and set it on the table beside her, afraid to hold it because his unexpected compliment had made her tremble.

'Why a Christmas candle?' she asked huskily.

'They're always slim and red.'

'And golden too, when they're alight. My hair is black.'

'But glowing. It doesn't have to be golden to give off light.'

He drew back a step, his mouth tightening as though afraid he had said too much, and Venetia picked up her juice and forced herself to sip some, hoping the quick beating of her heart would steady. Neil Adams' compliment was all the more surprising because she had never suspected him of regarding her as a woman. But it was unwise to read anything into his remark. He was a man and she was a good-looking girl. It was natural for him to notice it.

She glanced at him through the veil of her lashes. His mouth was set in a hard line and the muscles in his neck were taut. He was looking into his drink with the same intensity that she was pretending to look into hers, and she wondered again whether the cool detachment he exuded was a natural part of his make-up or a mask which he assumed to hide deeper, more uncontrollable emotions.

Quickly she turned her eyes away from him. They rested on a pile of records; Beethoven, Mozart, Chopin. The music the names evoked reverberated in her mind, reminding her that a man who could be moved to tears by the Sonata Pathétique could not be as immune to feelings as he pretended.

'Have you seen my wife since your return?'

The question startled her, but her training as a Press Officer came to her aid and she was able to look at him with a blank expression as she told him Margot was upstairs changing. Not knowing if he knew that his wife had been out with Boris Kanin, she was determined not to tell him herself, and was relieved when he accepted her bald answer and wandered over to look at his amplifier.

'I bought a couple of operas today,' he said. '*Norma* and *Otello*.'

'A jealous man and a jealous woman.' The words came out of their own volition, and though she regretted them she could not withdraw them.

'They both came to a sticky end,' he agreed. 'There's a moral in that somewhere!'

'One shouldn't be jealous,' she said promptly.

'Easier said than done.'

'What's easier said than done?' Margot spoke from the doorway, and then glided in on a cloud of Shalimar so pungent that Venetia sneezed.

'I'm sorry,' she apologised, and sneezed again. 'It's the scent.'

Margot looked contrite. 'I hadn't realised I'd put on so much.'

'I prefer it to the smell of peppermint,' Venetia smiled. Beside her there came a sharp intake of breath, then the shattering of glass as the tumbler in Neil Adams' hand fell to the marble hearth.

With a cry she leaned towards him. His face was white, but there was no sign of blood and she gave an embarrassed laugh. 'I thought you'd hurt yourself.'

'I leave that to others.'

Puzzled, she stared at him, and he shook his head as though telling her to go back to her chair. She did so, aware that Margot was watching them. She was also pale, and Venetia had the impression that behind this unimportant little drama lay something much deeper and uglier than she was able to guess.

'Let me pour you another pineapple juice, darling,' Margot said to her husband as she went to the cabinet.

'I'll do it myself.'

He did so, and Margot glided over to sit beside Venetia. 'If you sneeze again I'll go and change my dress. I must have dropped some perfume on the skirt.'

'My nose seems to have got used to it!'

'Perhaps you caught a cold this afternoon.' Margot glanced over her shoulder at her husband. 'Did you know Venetia had lunch with a devastating Chinese?'

'Miss Jackson has already told me.'

'I bet she didn't tell you she saw me and Boris lunching at the Mandarin too.'

The glass in the man's hand did not waver, but Venetia felt sure it was only kept steady by an enormous effort of will.

'Was it a good lunch?' he enquired casually.

'Marvellous, darling.' Margot's eyes gleamed with mischief. 'Boris ordered me something special and Russian.' She smiled at Venetia. 'His parents escaped during the Revolution and lived in Shanghai for years. He makes it sound a wonderful city. Such a pity the Chinese have got it now.'

The gong sounded and, still talking, Margot led the way to the dining room. Boris's parents, it seemed, had been able to smuggle out a great deal of their jewellery from Russia, which had enabled them to educate their son in Europe and America. He had eventually taken out American citizenship, but the lure of the Far East had brought him back to live in Hong Kong, where he had a flat overlooking the harbour.

'Small but convenient,' Margot concluded. 'He wasn't

brought up to luxury, like Neil and myself.'

'Eton wasn't luxury,' Neil interposed. 'If I remember rightly, I considered it a highly Spartan régime.'

'But if you'd had any children you would have sent them there, wouldn't you, darling?'

'It's pointless to discuss an academic question.'

'About non-existent children, you mean?' Margot turned to Venetia. 'I can't have any, you see, and Neil hates talking about it because he thinks it upsets me. But it doesn't. I never give it a thought.'

Venetia doubted this, for it was the second time in a week that Margot had deliberately brought up the subject of children. But why was she doing it in a way that was bound to hurt her husband? And succeeding, too, from the look on his face and the whiteness around his mouth.

Anxious to change the conversation, she brought it back to Boris Kanin, as being the lesser of the two evils. 'What does Mr Kanin do here?' she asked.

'He writes articles and does translations.'

Venetia hid her surprise. It seemed a mundane occupation for a man who looked as if he would be more at home hunting big game, possibly even killing them with his bare hands!

'He's looked after by a divine manservant,' Margot added. 'Completely hairless, with a scar down one cheek. They make a most sinister pair!'

'My wife enjoys the dramatic,' Neil Adams murmured.

'You're just jealous of Boris because he's so terribly attractive,' Margot pouted. 'All the men loathe him and all the women adore him.'

'Then no wonder we men don't like him,' Neil smiled, a movement of the lips that was in no way reflected by his expression. 'I had a letter from Sir William,' he said unexpectedly. 'He sends you his regards, Miss Jackson.'

'For heaven's sake call her Venetia,' Margot said irritably. 'We're not living in the nineteenth century!'

The fair hair gleamed in the light. 'If you have no objection——?'

Venetia shook her head and wondered if she would be expected to reciprocate. But he said nothing further, and wryly amused, she decided she was now doomed to wait until she caught his eye before she ever spoke to him.

'How is Sir William?' she asked hastily.

'As busy as ever. But he didn't refer to his health.'

'He never admits to a personal life at all,' she smiled.

'No wonder he and Neil get on so famously.' Margot reached out for a grape. She had eaten more tonight than at any time since Venetia's arrival, for she normally toyed with her food and seemed to exist on air. 'I've eaten so much it's made me tired,' she went on, almost as though she subconsciously guessed the thoughts coming from the other side of the table. 'I think I'll go to my room, if you'll both excuse me.'

'Would you like me to sit with you?' Venetia asked.

'When I want you to hold my hand I'll let you know.'

Red stained Venetia's high cheekbones, but she remained quiet as Margot sauntered out. No wonder the woman was tired. Boris Kanin would be a demanding and cruel lover; one only had to look at him to know that.

'I think I'll go to my room too.'

Venetia was on her feet and out of the room almost before her host had a chance to say goodnight. But as she reached the top of the stairs she paused and looked down into the hall. The dining room door was open, as she had left it in her precipitate flight, and light streamed out in a band of gold. She suddenly pictured Neil Adams sitting alone at the head of the table, fastidiously peeling a grape and giving no sign that he knew what Margot had been doing a few hours ago. Would he go to her room tonight too, or would the thought of Boris prevent him from doing so until tomorrow?

Abruptly she ran down the corridor to her bedroom. But once inside, the thoughts she was trying to escape came overwhelmingly to rest on her, and she was unable to push them away. Picking up a book, she tried to read, but it was impossible to concentrate. Writing letters home would be even more difficult and she did not bother to get out her pen. Perhaps she should go down to the library to finish her typing. Yet having pleaded tiredness it would look odd if she started to work. Restlessly she paced the floor. She could not face the prospect of going to bed and and lying there wakeful for hours, and she decided to try and walk off the unreasoning disquiet that pervaded her. Putting on a coat, she slipped quietly down the stairs and out of the house.

It was much colder than it had been during the day, and buttoning her collar tight, she set off along the winding road. Her high heels made it difficult to walk fast and she was annoyed that she had not had the foresight to change into lower ones. But it was too late to turn back and she pushed on steadily, pausing every so often to glance at the view, which was staggeringly beautiful. But walking was too uncomfortable for her to continue with her plan of climbing to the top of the Peak. The back of her heel was hurting and she stopped by a street lamp and leaned against it, the better to see if she had rubbed a blister. The faint light showed nothing other than redness, and she slipped her shoe on again and started to limp back the way she had come. As she did so a low-slung sports car came growling round the corner, its headlamps blazing. It came abreast of her, went past, and then stopped with a screech of brakes.

'Miss Jackson?' a deep voice called, and with embarrassment and dismay she saw Boris Kanin coming towards her. Blanched of all colour, he looked more simian than ever, his features brutal in their heaviness, his eyes as black as the hair which grew low over his forehead.

'Fate must indeed be smiling on me,' he said in his deep, fascinating voice. 'You've been in my thoughts all day, and now to meet you like this . . .' He flung out his hands in a gesture of pleasure, and then extended one to cup her elbow. 'You are going to the Peak to look at the view?'

'How did you guess?' she asked nervously.

'Because it is a pleasure I frequently give myself. I live down on the mid-level section. It gives me an excellent view of the harbour, but it is not the same as the view from the top.'

'I haven't managed to see it yet,' she confessed.

'Then I am glad I will be the one to show it to you.' He guided her to his car, a black Porsche with an engine of fierce power that would send it far ahead of other larger, more opulent-looking ones.

'You like it?' he asked, intercepting her glance at the bonnet.

'It's very compact and powerful.'

'Like me!'

'You'd be equally at home in a tank!'

'Do I strike you as being so ungainly?' he mocked.

'So overridingly determined to get your own way!'

He threw back his head and laughed, the muscles of his throat swelling with the sound. Standing in front of her, feet slightly apart, he needed only a fur hat to complete the picture emanated by his aura. No one would ever mistake Boris Kanin for an Englishman or a Latin. The virile force and chunky strength of him was unmistakably Mongol.

He drove in silence, concentrating on the road unwinding ahead of him like a curving ribbon. Higher and higher they climbed, the car hugging the road as though it loved the asphalt, the engine purring low and throatily, its power only half utilised. There were no other vehicles about and they seemed to be alone in a black and silver world.

The car stopped so smoothly that Venetia was taken unawares, and the man got out and came round to open the door for her. All his movements had the smoothness and ease of a panther, and like a panther he stood tense yet controlled beside her, giving the impression that he was waiting to spring. She shivered involuntarily, and he saw it and bent towards her.

'Are you cold? I'll give you my jacket.'

'No, thank you,' she said quickly. 'I'm fine.'

'But you shivered.'

'It was nothing.'

'I make you nervous.'

It was a statement rather than a question, and as such she decided to ignore it, and moved across the turf to have a better look at the view. They were at the highest point of the mountain, and far below the land appeared to float on a glittering jet sea, its undulating surface glinting silver in the light of a waning moon.

Beside her Venetia heard the man sigh. It was an unexpectedly soft sound from someone whom she considered to be the exact opposite, and she could not help a swift glance at him. He was staring at the horizon, his heavy profile looking as though it was carved of granite. She studied his mouth, both lips thin as a line, and the large nose that, jutting out from a low forehead, dominated the whole face. His eyes were half closed, the lids heavy and topped by thick black brows that looked as if they were unreal.

If he were aware of her scrutiny he gave no sign of it, but remained staring at the view, arms slack at his sides, his body teetering slowly backwards and forwards on the balls of his feet, almost as if he were a boxer who had been trained never to stand still.

'You can see now why I come up here,' he murmured, and turned to look her fully in the face.

She met his stare, though it took an effort, for she was determined not to let him know that she found his nearness worrying. How strong and self-confident he was, she thought, and wondered if he had always been the same. Somehow she could not imagine he had ever been weak or at a loss for words. Even as a child he must have been inviolate; set apart not only by his dark looks but by his air of command and strength. Or was it something other than humour? Certainly he gave the impression that he found the world amusing. It was apparent in his fearless stance and the mocking expression of his small dark eyes.

'Did you enjoy your lunch with Hoy?' he asked softly.

She was caught out by the question, for she had not known he was thinking of her.

'Yes, thank you.'

'Aren't you going to ask if I enjoyed mine?'

'Obviously you did. I don't think you're the sort of man who would do anything you didn't want to do.'

'Wanting to do something and enjoying it do not necessarily go together.'

'I think they would—with you.' Determined not to let him flirt with her, she looked him squarely in the face.

He returned the look with equal frankness and for a long moment their gazes held, though hers was the first to turn away.

'I must go back to the house,' she said.

'It's early yet. Let me take you out for a drink. I know an excellent place in Aberdeen.'

'Isn't that the section where all the fish restaurants are? And those beautiful boats on the water?'

'They are called junks,' he smiled. 'But haven't you been there yet? It must be remedied at once. We will go now.'

'Oh no,' she said hastily. 'I wasn't hinting. Anyway, I've already had dinner. It's half past nine, you know.'

'How late,' he mocked. 'I was forgetting the British always dine early.'

'So do half the people in the world.'

'The other half have no food to make dinner possible!'

His retort disconcerted her and she showed it, for his mouth curved in a smile, showing even white teeth, small and sharp as those of a fox.

'You never thought of that, did you, my fair Venetia?'

'No, Mr Kanin, I didn't.'

He chuckled. 'It will take more than your frigid little voice to put me in my place. Besides, I've no intention of calling you Miss Jackson, any more than I will allow you to go on calling me Mr Kanin. It's Boris.' His hands shot out to grip her arms. 'Say it,' he insisted. 'Say it.'

Coolly she did so, and again his teeth flashed in a smile.

'You sound like a Cox's apple,' he remarked. 'Sweet but very crisp!'

It was impossible not to laugh, and as he heard it, his hand slid down her arm to clasp her fingers. 'I am glad I can make you laugh, Venetia. I was beginning to doubt if I could.'

'Why are you flirting with me?' she demanded. 'I'm not your type.'

'How do you know?'

She was unwilling to reply, but he had no such inhibition and answered the question for her.

'You think I prefer frivolous socialities with more money than sense?'

'I didn't say that,' she protested.

'You didn't need to. Your thoughts were as clear as a neon sign!' He flung her a penetrating glance. 'But I'm not flirting with you, Venetia. With you, I say what I mean.'

'Do you ever?'

He did not dismiss the question but pondered over it, as though weighing up each word. 'I often lie,' he said finally. 'Not by what I say, but by what I omit to say. But with you I have not lied. From the moment I saw you this afternoon I wanted to take you away and——'

'Really, Mr Kanin, don't you think you're going too fast?'

'You do not like me to speak this way?'

'I find it childish.' She dug her hands into the pockets of her coat. 'We hardly know each other. Besides, you're a friend of Mrs Adams.' She paused. 'A very good friend.'

'We are lovers,' he said deliberately.

Venetia caught her breath at the frank admission. Yet had she given it any previous thought she would have realised a man like Boris Kanin would not bother with the mores of social convention. But even if he eschewed convention for himself, surely he had some respect for Margot's position?

'You're not very gallant, are you, Mr Kanin?'

'Boris,' he reminded her, and then said: 'I am being honest with you. I think you are a person who would prefer that.'

'Naturally I like honesty. But not when it destroys someone else's privacy.'

'It is no secret on the Island about Margot and myself. Everyone knows, including her husband.'

It was confirmation of what she had suspected. Her momentary hope that Neil Adams might not have known what was going on, flickered and died, and with it died her respect for him. How could one have respect for a cuckolded husband!

'I am sorry my frankness disturbs you,' Boris said. 'But I do not wish to start our friendship on a false premise.'

'We cannot be friends, Mr Kanin. I have no intention of seeing you again.'

'Don't talk like a fool!'

She marched back to the car. 'Your attentions disgust me, and so does your loyalty to Margot!'

'You have an old-fashioned notion of what a love affair is.' He was beside the car, holding open the door for her to get in. 'Two people meet and are attracted to one another. Fifty years ago they would have exchanged visiting cards and a couple of dances. Today they go to bed. When it is over, it is forgotten.'

She thought of the scarlet mouth and flushed face that she had seen earlier that evening, and knew that though he might forget, Margot would not forget him.

'Please drive me home, Mr Kanin. And if you're looking for a replacement for Mrs Adams, I suggest you tell her and cast your net in another direction.'

He released the brake and they glided down the slope, going several yards before he switched on the ignition. The engine trembled and it was as though blood was surging through the body of the car, giving it the power to go faster. Down the road they went and round the sharp bends with a turn of speed that made her scalp prickle and the brakes shriek their protest. The man was crouched over the wheel, hands gripping the rim, eyes peering intently through the windscreen as he kept his foot hard on the accelerator and then harder still on the brake.

Venetia was flung first forward and then back again, and would almost have gone through the windscreen had it not been for the protection of her safety belt. That he was trying to scare her she had no doubt, nor that he was doing so because of what she had said to him, but she had no intention of apologising for it, nor of doing anything to make him think she had changed her mind. The man was insufferable, and she would be even ruder to him if he gave her the chance.

Within moments the lights of the Adams' house glimmered ahead of her. 'You needn't bother going into the drive,' she said, but he took no notice and brought the car to a squealing stop at the front of the steps.

He bounded from it with an agile movement and was at her side to help her out before she could prevent him, holding her elbow between fingers of steel. Together they walked up the steps and were halfway to the door when Neil Adams opened it.

Venetia turned scarlet. He was the last man she wanted to see now, but there was no backing away from his cold scrutiny.

'I wondered who was arriving so late,' he said. 'I hadn't realised you had gone out, Miss Jackson. I thought you were in bed.'

'I wanted some fresh air, so I—I went for a walk. I met Mr Kanin by accident.'

'I showed Venetia the view from the Peak.' Boris's voice was tinged with humour, as were his eyes when he looked at her. 'Don't forget our drink together. I will call you.' He ran lightly down to the car, and with the minimum of movement swung it round in a tight circle and shot into the darkness.

Venetia was uncomfortably aware of Neil Adams beside her, his entire presence exuding displeasure. 'I didn't know Mr Kanin was a friend of yours too,' he said.

'He isn't. I met him by accident.'

'On the way to the Peak?' There was disbelief in the

question, and she reacted to it with a surge of anger that he should doubt her word.

'I'm tired, Mr Adams, I'm going to my room.'

'You were tired before,' he said pointedly. 'Or is this your way of telling me you have an assignation with someone else!'

'Oh, stop using such old-fashioned words!' she said crossly. 'I told you—I met him by accident.'

'Are you asking me to believe it's an accident that within a week of being here you know the two most notorious bachelors in the Colony?'

'I'm not asking you to believe anything,' she stormed. 'But I'd like you to remember that I'm single and free! Now if you'd kindly get out of my way ...'

'I don't want you to see Kanin again.'

The order caught her as she stepped past him, and she stopped and swung round. 'What right do you have to tell me who my friends should be?'

'Because of my position with the Government,' he replied coldly. 'It is the reason you were sent here.'

'What has your position got to do with Boris Kanin?'

'He's a Russian.'

'Being Russian doesn't make him a spy!'

'You are not to see him,' Neil Adams insisted, his mouth rigid with disapproval. 'Do I make myself clear?'

'Very clear,' she retorted, 'but is it clear to your wife? Or don't your orders apply to *her*?'

'My wife——' He stopped and his mouth set even more firmly. 'She resents being told what to do. She is highly strung. I have to treat her carefully.'

'Does that mean looking the other way?'

The silence was electric and the air between them seemed to crackle. Venetia regretted the words but had no intention of apologising for them. How dared he be such a harsh judge of her behaviour, yet allow Margot to make such a fool of him?

'I cannot control what my wife does,' he said bleakly, 'but *you* were sent to make my task easier.'

'I don't see how my friendship with Mr Hoy or Mr Kanin can made it *harder* for you. If your dislike of them is purely personal—and I can understand why you resent Mr Kanin,' she said carefully, 'it still doesn't give you the right to tell me how I should spend my free time.'

'Then you won't listen to me?' he said with a harshness she had never heard before.

'Not until your wife does!'

He took a step forward and the light streaming out from the hall illumined the shine of sweat on his forehead. For all his iron control he was unable to prevent this tell-tale give-away of his feelings, and seeing it, some of her anger evaporated, leaving her again uncomfortably aware of a little-boy-lost quality about him that was at variance with his icily detached manner.

'I don't want to quarrel with you, Mr Adams,' she said quickly, 'but I won't let you treat me like a child, nor can I pretend to be one. I came here because Sir William asked me to, but'—she hesitated, and moistened her lips before she continued—'but I wouldn't have come if I had known it was going to be so difficult. I'm not sure it wouldn't be better for everyone concerned if you *did* allow your wife to return to England. It would solve a lot of problems.'

'If Margot returns so must I. I will not let her go home alone. I must be with her.'

For no reason she could define, the words depressed Venetia, indicating as they did his depth of love. Only deep emotion could make a man of Neil Adams' reserve make such a disclosure.

'Do you think being with her will help you to keep her?' she blurted out. 'Don't you think it might be better if you stood up to her more?'

'You are in no position to judge my actions,' he said icily.

'I've been here long enough to see what's going on.' Anger made her reckless. 'I know I haven't the right to talk to you like this, but we've both been pretty frank with each other tonight. I can't stand by and watch you being made a fool of.'

'You are indeed frank, Venetia.' He used her Christian name for the first time and she trembled as she heard it. He made it sound so different, accenting each syllable and giving them all equal weight. 'But being witness to a situation doesn't make you a good judge of it. Margot and I have been married for ten years. They have not been easy years, but we are bound to each other and nothing can alter that.'

The tone in which he spoke, as well as the context, gave Venetia food for thought, but it did not take her long to digest the meaning.

'Are you tied for religious reasons?'

'No.'

'Then why——?'

He averted his head. 'No matter what Margot says or does, she will always return to me.'

'And you will always be waiting?'

'Yes.'

Tears filled Venetia's eyes and her voice was bleak. 'You must love her very much.'

'We have digressed from our original conversation.' He still kept his face averted. 'I hope you will do as I have asked.'

'Not unless you give me a better reason than prejudice.'

She waited for his reply, then accepting the fact that he had no intention of making one, she opened the door wider. 'If you wish me to return to England, Mr Adams, I will be quite happy to do so.'

'I wouldn't be at all happy for you to go.'

She was startled. 'Even though I won't listen to you?'

'Perhaps I shouldn't have demanded it.'

His climb-down startled her even more. Had his earlier desire to control her actions stemmed from fury that he was unable to control his wife? It was a logical assumption and one which, highlighting the weakness in his character, disturbed her.

'You'd better forget what I said.' He was speaking again, his voice brisker than usual. 'And I'll forget what *you* said.'

'It might be better if you remembered it.'

'I have enough to remember with regret,' he replied, 'without remembering this too.'

With a murmured goodnight, he walked down the steps. Oblivious to the cold wind blowing, she watched him till he was out of sight, then went into the hall and closed the door, careful not to latch it.

What a strange man he was, and what a strange marriage he had. How destructive love could be if it could force a man of pride to humble himself; if it could make him deaf to the truth and blind to reality. How could he say Margot needed him when she so patently didn't? Even more important, why was he so sure that if she left him she would return? Was it his way of saying it had happened before?

Slowly Venetia climbed the stairs. Today two men had made it plain that they were attracted to her, yet ironically her thoughts centred on the one man who did not see her at all.

'Except as a means of keeping his wife with him,' she murmured aloud. 'So put that in your pipe and smoke it, Venetia Jackson!'

CHAPTER SEVEN

WHEN Venetia went into Margot's bedroom the next morning, complete with details of the seating plan for the Women's League charity luncheon to be held at the Peninsula Hotel, she found Margot on the telephone. She went to leave the room, but the other woman beckoned her to remain, and she sat down, the papers in her lap.

She only needed to hear a few words to know Boris was on the other end of the line. Margot did not hide the warmth in her voice, nor the slumbrous look in her eyes.

'Darling, I can't,' she was saying. 'I told you yesterday I wouldn't be able to come. I have this luncheon today and Neil will expect me to be in to dinner.' Margot's head tilted to one side as she pressed the receiver more closely to her ear. Slowly the look of complacency vanished from her face and it became hard and ugly.

Venetia found it astonishing that a change of expression could so materially affect someone's looks. It was like seeing a beautiful flower wither in front of her eyes.

'You're not to do it,' Margot ordered, her voice high. 'You know how I feel ... Very well, tonight, then! But not before eight.' The receiver clattered to rest and Margot shifted on her pillows to look at Venetia. 'You don't believe in letting the grass grow under your feet, do you?'

Bewildered, Venetia did not know what to say. Not that she would have been given any opportunity for saying it even if she had, for Margot let forth a tirade of anger that left Venetia equally angry in return.

What on earth had possessed Boris to tell Margot he had taken her to the Peak last night? Although she had only heard one side of the telephone conversation, she knew it had not slipped out by accident. He had deliberately said it in order to bring Margot to heel.

'My meeting with Mr Kanin was an accident,' she said, cutting through Margot's outburst.

'You know he lives near here.'

'I thought he lived near the harbour. I can assure you I would have enjoyed my walk much more had I *not* seen him.'

'It's a pity you didn't give *him* that impression! You went up to the Peak with him.'

'I was going there and he offered me a lift. It would have been rude to have refused it.'

'You'd better be rude next time, then—if there is a next time.' There was still an ugly expression on Margot's face. 'I don't mind sharing most things with you, Venetia, but Boris isn't one of them!'

'I've no desire to share anything with you,' Venetia retorted coldly. 'I think it would be best if I returned to England.'

'Don't be silly.' Margot's voice was so melodious it was hard to believe it had ever been strident with anger. 'You should have got used to my temper by now. You know what I'm like in the morning.'

And in the afternoon and evening too, when the mood takes you, Venetia thought to herself, but decided there was no point saying so. Criticism would not affect Margot's behaviour.

'I don't think I'm cut out for this kind of work,' was all Venetia said out loud. 'I'll stay until you find someone else.'

'I've no intention of letting you go. You're the nicest person I've had working for me and I hope you'll stay with me when we get back to England. Come and sit beside me and show me the table plan.' Margot patted the bed and Venetia moved slowly across to it.

Though unmollified by the apology, she knew better than to reiterate what she had just said, and decided to talk to Neil Adams instead. After all, it was his request that had brought her here, and she could not leave until he allowed her to do so. At least not if she wanted to go on working at the Foreign Office.

Forcing herself to a calmness she did not feel, she went through the table plans. The luncheon was being given to raise money for an old people's home, a problem which, until the last couple of years, had not been of great importance in the Colony. With their veneration for age and their strong sense of family, very few elderly Chinese had need of public aid. No matter how straitened the circumstances of a son or daughter, room was always made for a parent—sometimes both—when they became too old to manage on their own. But this pattern was now changing. Accommodation was at a premium and two-roomed flats would frequently house families with four or more children. With such cramped accommodation the normal life style was slowly being changed too, and more and more old folk were finding that their children—no matter how willing to have them—simply did not have the space. The obvious solution was an old people's home, and though the first one had taken a long time to fill—not because of lack of old people, but because pride would not let them admit their families were unable to have them—once a few rooms were occupied, the rest filled up, and the waiting list was soon so long that more homes became a priority. Margot had been co-opted on to one of the committees concerned with such a project, but usually tried to avoid as many meetings as she could.

'Neil's desperately anxious for me to be occupied,' she had once said. 'The poor darling has spent all our marriage trying to keep me busy.'

In view of Margot's last conversation with Boris, Venetia was more than ready to concede that Neil Adams was wasting his time. A woman of Margot's temperament could not be coerced into a position she did not want to occupy, and there was no doubting her unwillingness to live up to her present commitments. It was a pity Neil did not accept the inevitable and allow his wife to return to England and live her own life; even perhaps to give her the freedom she so obviously wanted.

'You must come to the luncheon too,' Margot interrupted

Venetia's thoughts, and picking up a pencil, she scratched a large 'V' into a seat that was still vacant.

'A ticket costs fifty Hong Kong dollars,' Venetia said hastily. 'I don't mind giving ten to a good cause, but I can't afford fifty.'

'Neil will pay,' came the careless answer. 'He wants me to have a social secretary, so he must keep her happy.'

'I'll be perfectly happy to have lunch here!'

'Well, I won't. Besides, it's my way of apologising to you for losing my temper. I didn't mean it, Venetia, but I'm so jealous of Boris...'

Margot flung aside the bedclothes and went to stand by the window, careless of the sunshine streaming through it and dissolving the opacity of her nightdress. Her figure could be seen as clearly as though she was wearing nothing. It was a lovely figure: too thin, but with a delicacy of line that reminded Venetia of a Degas drawing. She tried to picture what Margot had looked like ten years ago when she had first married, and could understand why a man would want to possess her. Even today, capricious and petulant though she was, she still possessed a charm that could blind you. How much stronger it must have been before boredom with life had laid its mark on her character. Visualising the shimmering radiance and vividness of a young Margot, it was easy to see why she had appealed to the silver-blond man who still so patently adored her.

Venetia was not conscious of sighing, and only as she heard the sudden expulsion of breath did she know she had done so. Why should Neil Adams' love for his wife distress her? She couldn't be jealous. The thought was so ridiculous that she pushed it away instantly. But if it was not jealousy, what was it? Maybe her sadness stemmed from knowing that even a deep love could not always arouse the right response. She might even be reacting to the man's inner loneliness. For that he *was* lonely she had no doubt. The impression of coldness and detachment which he gave was only a mask to hide feelings that were completely to the contrary.

'You look very disapproving, Venetia.' Margot glided back and picked up a negligee. 'Don't you like me wandering around like this?'

Venetia smiled. 'I've no objection to anyone showing off a beautiful body. It's only ugly ones that need to be hidden.'

'Thank goodness I don't need to hide mine yet.' Margot went to the dressing-table. 'They always say you lose your figure if——' she stopped. 'But I still have mine.' She bent close to the glass and peered at her face. 'My looks don't pity me,' she said. 'They never have.'

'You talk as if your looks are hiding something,' Venetia said. 'Have you been ill?'

'I was born with one skin too few.' Margot swung round, her blue eyes narrowed. 'You're far too phlegmatic and withdrawn to know what that means.'

'It means you have heightened emotion and awareness,' Venetia said matter-of-factly. 'You might consider me a very dull potato, but I do know what it means to have one skin less!'

Margot laughed, the sound bubbling up in her so that she looked unexpectedly happy. 'I'm not surprised I like you, Venetia, you keep me on my toes.' She turned back to the mirror again. 'Yes, I have got one skin too few. My black moods are blacker than anyone else's and my bright moods blind me.'

'I should imagine they blind others too,' Venetia said drily. 'You're a man-eater.'

'You disapprove of my friendship with Boris, don't you?' Margot did not wait for an answer. 'Don't judge me the way you do other people. There's so much you don't know about me ... so much you can't——' She turned to the mirror again, hands trembling visibly as she picked up a brush and ran it through her rich red hair. 'What do you think of my darling Russian?'

'Does it matter what I think?'

'Why don't you like him?'

'A few moments ago you said I was out to trap him!'

85

'I only said that in a temper. But you don't like him, do you?'

'I neither like him nor dislike him,' said Venetia. 'He's a—I've never met anyone of his type before.'

'What type do you think he is?'

'I'm not sure. But he's very strong and cruel and very conscious of his power over women.'

'He has every right to be,' Margot said drily. 'He just has to look at them and they immediately go horizontal!'

Venetia flushed. She was not unused to plain speaking on matters of sex, but there was a difference between the chaff and raillery of a light flirtation, and the raw passion for Boris which Margot made no attempt to hide.

'How shockable you are!' Margot chided. 'No wonder Boris wanted to flirt with you. He's always found virgins exciting!'

'How are we going to get these seating plans to the hotel?' Venetia said, standing up and gathering her papers together. 'If you'd given them to me yesterday I could have posted them off, but——'

'I had migraine, remember?' Margot said coldly. 'You couldn't expect me to work when I couldn't lift my head from the pillow.'

'Of course not.' Venetia was contrite. 'What I really meant was that I'd better take them there myself.'

'A good idea. Get dressed for the lunch and go. I'll meet you at the hotel at noon.'

'I don't really think I should attend,' Venetia put in.

'For heaven's sake, don't argue about it.'

Not wishing to arouse Margot's temper again, Venetia left.

An hour later, wearing a simple yet well-cut dress and jacket of fine lemon wool that accentuated the jet black of her hair, she was walking along Salisbury Road to the Peninsula Hotel. More old-fashioned-looking than the Mandarin, it could easily have passed for a Royal residence in the Victorian era, and could just as easily have been standing on the plains of India as facing the waters of

Victoria Harbour. The atmosphere of the lobby was old-fashioned too, with potted palms, round tables covered with stiff white cloths and large yet comfortable-looking chairs. Not for the Peninsula Hotel the brash bustle of its rivals. Here the atmosphere was calmer and more staid, although there seemed to be an equal number of tourists and camera-clutching Japanese.

Making her way to the first floor, Venetia was directed to the suite where the luncheon was being held, and giving her plans to the pretty Chinese girl in charge, found herself with an hour to spare.

She decided to look around Kowloon. It was far more interesting to window-shop here than on the island of Hong Kong, which contained more offices, banks and shipping companies than shops, though it did have many jewellery ones, whose prices—despite Hong Kong being a no-duty port—were astonishingly high for her pocket. But the stores in Kowloon were for the most part small Aladdin's Caves filled with a plethora of goods: bags, shoes, gloves, dresses, coats, all guaranteed to attract the most jaded eye. Indeed, after walking down Hankow Road and several side streets, she could not absorb any more, so satiated was she by the vast amount of articles begging to be bought, and was glad to return to the Peninsula Hotel, arriving at the front entrance at the same time as a dark limousine deposited Margot by the steps.

She was soignée in a severe black suit, her beautiful hair covered by a small hat with eye-touching veil. Looking at her it was difficult to believe she could ever lose her temper or say things that could wound so deeply, and Venetia could well understand why she was so sought after by the English people living here, who considered it a favour when Margot deigned to grace their functions or preside over their bridge and cocktail parties.

During the luncheon her mask of affability did not slip once. Not only was she Mrs Neil Adams, but she also was Margot Destry, the beautiful assured daughter of a noble line. Her speech of thanks at the end of the luncheon to all the women who had paid so highly for their tickets was a masterly display of conciseness and wit, and not until they were driving back in the car did the mask slip and the lovely face show signs of irritation.

'How smug those women were!' she exclaimed, pulling off her hat and running slim fingers through her hair. 'They're all so contented with their lot. So narrow-minded and prissy!'

'Not so narrow-minded that they're unwilling to help other people,' Venetia replied.

'Do you see good in everybody?' It was a petulant question.

'I try to.'

'I bet you were head girl in your school.'

'I'm afraid I was!'

Unexpectedly Margot laughed, her good humour restored, and she leaned back and flung off her shoes, wriggling her toes in the thick pile of the carpet. 'Why don't you go out with Simon Hoy tonight?' she suggested. 'Neil and I will both be out and you'll be alone in the house.'

'I'll have an early night.'

Margot shrugged and, duty done, looked uninterestedly through the window. She seemed to be lost in her own thoughts and Venetia, replete from an excellent lunch, dozed beside her.

Arriving at the house, Margot drifted away, murmuring that she did not want to be disturbed, and Venetia decided to finish the backlog of typing still to be done, and when this was completed, rattled off a letter to Sir William. It was unwise to tell him all her thoughts regarding her position here, but she left him in no doubt that she might not be able to stay until the negotiations with the Chinese had been completed.

'I feel as though I'm walking on a tightrope,' she wrote, 'and that at any moment it will either break or be cut through.'

Only as she read the letter back did this particular phrase strike her as strange. What had made her put it like that?

There was no doubt she was walking a tightrope that might break, but why should she fear it might be cut? What sinister presence did she sense that gave her the feeling that disaster might not only come of its own accord, but be deliberately caused?

And if so, by whom?

Simon Hoy? His name flashed into her mind. It was more than likely he was not as sanguine as he pretended about the future of his business should the trade talks with the Chinese prove successful, though she could not imagine him doing anything active to upset them. Yet when people felt their livelihood threatened they were apt to do strange things, and though she knew he was extremely rich, she was worldly enough to know that great wealth did not preclude the desire for even greater wealth.

She pushed back her chair and put the cover over her typewriter, wishing she could as easily mask her thoughts. But the disquiet inside her could not be covered, and it remained with her as she went upstairs to bathe and change for dinner.

Standing by the mirror in her bathcoat a little later, she debated whether to have supper in her room, but the thought of going to bed made her more dejected than she already was, and determined to fight it, she decided to wear one of her prettiest dresses: full-skirted red velvet that made her skin gleam like a pearl. She brushed her hair until it shone like ebony, then drew it away from her face into a coil on her neck. The severe style showed off her broad forehead and the winging eyebrows that curved gracefully over wide-apart sea-green eyes.

Skirts trailing behind her, she went down to the drawing-room. Alone there, she savoured the lovely furniture and wondered what it looked like in its own setting, and whether it came from Neil Adams' town house—which she knew to be in Westminster—or from his home in the country, the lovely grey stone mansion she had glimpsed in the snapshot. She wandered over to the sideboard and stared at the array of bottles on the silver tray: orangeade, lemonade, tomato juice and pineapple. Even though neither of the Adams liked to drink, it was strange they did not cater for their guests. Not that I'm a guest, she reminded herself, and filling a tumbler with tonic water, carried it over to the hearth.

She settled herself in a wing chair. A quarter to eight. At this time in London she would probably be on her way out to dinner, or else dining with friends in her flat; certainly not sitting alone wondering how to pass the evening. Her job in the Press office had given her a hectic working, as well as social life, for many of the people she met during the day were her friends in the evening. Darn Beeby! He would have a hard time persuading her to do him another favour when she got back to England!

Restlessly she jumped up and walked round the room. It was a pity she couldn't return home at once. Remaining here was both claustrophobic and unnerving, and she knew an intense desire to escape.

'Running away from your thoughts?'

A deep voice set her spinning on her heel to see Boris Kanin coming towards her. In a black mohair silk suit he looked more swarthy than ever, his jowls and chin blue where he had shaved, his black brows beetling over his narrow eyes.

'You look beautiful,' he murmured, not waiting for her to reply. 'You should always wear red.'

'It matches my mood,' she retorted.

'Scarlet for passion?'

'And anger. Why did you tell Margot you saw me last night?'

'Why shouldn't I have?'

'Because a clever man never lets one woman know he's seen another—unless he wants to create mischief.'

He chuckled. 'I am a mischievous man. Anyway, what does it matter if she knows?'

'Because I don't like being used! And you used *me* to force Margot to go out with you tonight!'

'If I hadn't used you,' he shrugged, 'I would have found

something else with which to provoke her. She's easy to provoke, that one.'

Venetia choked with anger. 'Haven't you any loyalty—any decency? How can you talk about her like that?'

'Don't be trite.'

Furiously she backed away, but he caught her by the shoulder and pulled her close. His eyes looked more red than brown, and seemed to be on fire.

'No woman turns away from me,' he said savagely, and clamped his mouth down hard on hers.

There was nothing unexpected in his kiss. It was exactly as she knew him to be: ruthless, dominant, passionate. Instinctively she knew that to resist him would only inflame him the more, and she remained quiescent, her mouth motionless beneath his, her teeth clamped tightly together.

Slowly he drew back and looked at her. 'Don't pretend you're an ice-maiden,' he said suavely.

'I wouldn't dream of pretending with you, Mr. Kanin.'

'Then why the frigid act?'

'I don't warm to you.' Her eyes were mocking. 'You're not my type.'

A flicker of anger crossed his face and she knew a momentary triumph. For all his assurance he did not like to be rebuffed.

'Who *is* your type?' he demanded. 'The affable young Chinese or the effete Neil Adams?'

'I find them both more attractive than you.'

'Perhaps you're more afraid of me?' His head bent and though he did not touch her, she felt his breath warm on her skin. 'It would take very little for me to break you, Venetia.'

Deliberately she moved away from him. 'Would you care for a tonic water, Mr Kanin?'

'Make it strychnine,' he grunted. 'I'm sure you'd enjoy pouring that for me!'

Despite herself she laughed, and the sound still echoed in the room as she saw Neil Adams cross the hall and go upstairs. Venetia forced herself to concentrate on the man in front of her.

'I don't dislike you enough to hang for you, Mr Kanin.'

'Call me Boris and I'll be more likely to believe it!' He perched on the arm of the chair. For such a broad, thickset man he moved with astonishing grace, and she wondered what exercises he did to keep himself so physically in trim.

'Why must you go out with Margot?' she asked abruptly. 'You're just amusing yourself with her, aren't you?'

It was not a question she had intended to ask, but the sight of Neil had made her aware of the delicate balance of his marriage. Expecting Boris to tell her to mind her own business, she was disconcerted to see him smile. But then he probably enjoyed discussing his conquests. His answer said as much.

'If it were not me, Margot would find someone else. She is a peach waiting to be plucked. So ripe, in fact,' he said with a sly grin, 'that she would have fallen into any man's hands! Obviously her husband keeps his hands to himself!'

'How crude you are!'

'Life *is* crude, Venetia, and women like Margot only prove my point. Her husband doesn't satisfy her, so she goes looking elsewhere. She is only concerned with herself. She doesn't care how much she hurts anyone else.'

'Neither do you. You're not in love with her, but you're using her.'

His look was sharp. 'What use is she to me?'

'She's a beautiful and well-known Englishwoman,' Venetia said coldly. 'It must satisfy your ego to be seen with her.'

'Russian peasant with an English aristocrat?' His smile was wolfish. 'That sort of thinking is dead as the dodo!'

Knowing he was right, she reddened. 'You make me sound like a snob, Mr Kanin, and I'm not.'

'I believe that.' He got to his feet. 'But that's all I believe about you.'

'What do you mean?'

'The rest of the picture you've built up is false. You are not the type to be a social secretary. You have too much initiative and drive.'

'The job requires initiative and drive.'

'If you were working for a Vanderbilt, possibly, but not for poor Margot. She is a butterfly winging her way from candle to candle, and you, I think, were brought here to see she doesn't singe her wings.'

'You'd make a superb novelist, Mr Kanin. You should try and create another James Bond.'

'I have,' he smiled. 'Me!'

Before she could think of a suitably crushing reply, Margot came in, breathtakingly lovely in black chiffon, her hair glowing like a flame. Sparing only a brief glance at Venetia, she pulled Boris from the room, and a moment later an engine revved and then faded into the distance.

Venetia sighed; the tightrope she was walking appeared to be fraying beneath her feet. If Margot continued to be so brazen in her relationship with Boris, even Neil would not be able to go on tolerating it. It was not easy to forestall gossip in a big city, but in a place like Hong Kong it was impossible. If the talks with the Chinese would be doomed by Neil's premature departure, then Sir William might just as well accept their failure now, for with all the will in the world Venetia could not see the present situation continuing much longer.

The Chinese butler hovered by the door, his face inscrutable as he told her dinner was ready. She crossed towards the dining room, and as she did so, heard a step on the stairs. She stopped, her heart beating fast as she saw Neil Adams.

'I—I thought you'd gone out,' she stammered.

'I'm just leaving.'

He came down the last step. Expecting him to look different, she was surprised that he looked the same, as reserved as always, his face pale and expressionless. Didn't he care that his wife was out with another man, and was he so little a man himself that he could accept such a situation?

'I'm sorry you have to dine alone, Venetia, I hadn't realised Margot would be out. I expressly asked her to stay in.'

'There's no reason why I shouldn't dine alone. Staff generally do.'

'You're not staff,' he said sharply, and came to a stop in front of her. As usual he was immaculately dressed, though in a black suit and not a dinner jacket. Aware of what was going through her mind, he said: 'I'm dining with some Chinese officials and they always wear tunics.' He hesitated. 'They have flown in from Peking.'

'When do you think your talks will be completed?' she asked.

'I'm not sure. Possibly far sooner than I had anticipated. Why do you ask?'

'Because I don't want to stay here. I find the job more—more tedious than I thought I would.'

'Don't you mean more difficult?'

She nodded. 'But I won't leave without your permission, of course.'

'Then you must be prepared to stay here until my work is finished!' His voice was as bleak as her expression. 'If you can bring yourself to accept that, Venetia, it will help you to settle down more easily.'

'Don't you think I haven't tried to settle down? But I can't. I'm irritated and bored!'

'With two men willing to dance attendance on you?' His look was bleaker still. 'I'm sure Mr Kanin will be willing to oblige when Mr Hoy is unavailable.'

'Don't judge me by your wife's standards,' she flared.

'Don't judge my wife!' he rapped back.

'How can I help it? I live in your house and I can see what's going on!' Her eyes met his, and as she saw the pain in them a strange pang went through her. 'I know why you want me to stay, but—but don't you think it would be better if you allowed Margot to return to England?'

'I told you before that I have no intention of being separated from my wife.' His voice was as cold and icy as the water from a mountain stream. 'I have never attached importance to gossip and I don't care what people say about me. Only if their remarks affect my work will I then do anything to stop it. Do you understand what I mean?'

'I'm afraid I don't.'

He sighed and she knew that though he was going to explain, he regretted having to do so. 'I specifically asked Sir William to find me someone trustworthy to stay with Margot. I am not just anxious to prevent her doing something she might regret for herself, but to stop her from doing anything to lower my status with the Chinese.' He paused. 'Like the Japanese, they are very concerned over loss of face.'

She began to have an idea of what he was trying to say. 'You mean that if a man can't control his wife, they consider he has lost face?'

'Yes. And if they suspected that has happened to me, my position as negotiator would be weakened.'

'Surely they don't think your personal life affects your professional one?'

'A man who is weak with his wife is a weak man,' he explained.

'A man isn't his brother's keeper,' she retorted. 'Nor his wife's either!'

'The Chinese would disagree with you.'

'Then wouldn't you lose less face if you allowed Margot to go home?'

'I have to be with her,' he said harshly. 'I've already told you that. If she goes, I go.'

'Then you *are* weak,' she burst out, 'and no woman loves a man who clings to her! If you want your wife to love you, you should——'

'She hates me!' The words were torn from him. 'Surely you're aware of that?'

Venetia floundered, not knowing what to say. 'Not

hatred ... surely not. I mean, she's sarcastic ... sometimes cruel ... but I—I thought it was a sophisticated way of talking.'

'She means it,' he said. 'Every word.'

'And you still won't let her go?'

Without answering he picked up his coat from a chair and walked out.

Only as the front door closed behind him did she go into the dining room and, for the butler's sake, make a pretence of eating. Dinner over, she took a stroll in the grounds, but it had grown cold and she was glad to return to the centrally-heated warmth of the library where she played a few records and tried not to think of anything. But it was difficult to keep her mind blank, and at ten o'clock she went to bed.

Even here she could not relax, and she tossed and turned the tedious hours away. The house was quiet, and apart from the servants she knew herself to be alone in it, for neither Margot nor Neil had returned. She sat up and switched on the light. Two-thirty. It was later than she had realised and sleep was no nearer than it had been at midnight. Deciding that a glass of hot milk might soothe her, she put on her dressing gown and padded downstairs.

A few lamps had been left turned on, and they shed small pools of light along the corridors and hall. But entering the kitchen she found the fluorescent tubes gleaming, and saw Neil's Chinese manservant stirring something on the gas stove.

He shuffled forward to greet her, anxiously enquiring if anything was wrong. He was an old man with a mass of tiny lines criss-crossing his yellow skin and making it look like crumpled parchment. But his eyes were bright and alert, and though she had only spoken to him rarely, she knew he was intelligent and perceptive.

'I couldn't sleep,' she said in answer to his question, 'so I came down for some milk.' She wandered over to peer into the wok standing over the flame. It was a bowl-shaped pan which, together with a steamer, seemed to comprise

Mills & Boon

Love, romance, intrigue...
all are captured for you
by Mills & Boon's top-selling authors.

Take four exciting books FREE every month

Also FREE – a fashionable canvas bag.

NO STAMP NEEDED

FREE BOOKS CERTIFICATE

Send to: Mills & Boon Reader Service, P.O. Box 236, Thornton Road, Croydon, Surrey CR9 9EL.

Please send me my first parcel of the twelve latest Mills & Boon books and my free tote bag – I would like to subscribe for six months. Each month I will receive twelve brand new romances, postage and packing free. I understand that you will invoice me for the cost of eight books at £8.80 and that the other four books will be ABSOLUTELY FREE. If I decide not to subscribe, I shall return the first twelve books to you within 10 days and owe nothing. If I decide to subscribe, I understand that after six months I may cancel my subscription at any time simply by writing to you. I am over 18 years of age. Please write in BLOCK CAPITALS.

Name _____ Signature _____

Address _____

_____ Postcode _____

Please don't forget to include your postcode. Orders returned without a signature will not be accepted. One offer per household. Offer applies in U.K. only, overseas send for details. If price changes are necessary you will be notified. *Offer expires 30.9.84*

8 + 4   **SEND NO MONEY – TAKE NO RISKS**   3R4BP

A sensational offer to readers of Mills & Boon the world's largest publisher of romantic fiction.

Receive twelve marvellous romances each month – but only pay for eight.

Yes, it's true. Accept this offer, subscribe to Mills & Boon for just six months, and you w receive four of the latest, brand new titles each month, absolutely **free!**

And you can enjoy many other advantages:

- **POSTAGE & PACKING FREE** – unlike other boo clubs, we pay all the extras.
- **FREE MONTHLY NEWSLETTER** – keeps you up to date with all the new books plus offers you the chance to save even more money with special bargain book offers.
- **HELPFUL FRIENDLY SERVICE** – from the girls at Mills & Boon. You can ring them anytime on 01-684 2141.
- **THE NEWEST ROMANCES** – all twelve books in your monthly parcel (including the Four Free titles) are the very latest titles which are reserved for you at the printers and delivered t you hot off the press by Mills and Boon.

FREE BAG
Our exclusive white canvas tote bag with the Mills & Boon symbol – yours FREE – whatever you decide!

10 DAY TRIAL FREE

It's so easy! Send no money now – you don't even neec a stamp. Just fill in and detach the reply card and send it off today.

Should you change your mind about subscribing, simply return your first twelve books to u within 10 days and you will owe nothing. The tote bag is yours to keep – whatever yo decide.

Mills & Boon Reader Service, P.O. Box 236, Thornton Road, Croydon. Surrey. CR9 3R

Postage will be paid by Mills & Boon Limited

Do not affix postage stamps if posted in Gt. Britain, Channel Islands or N. Ireland.

BUSINESS REPLY SERVICE
Licence No. CN 81

Mills & Boon Reader Service,
PO Box 236, Thornton Road,
CROYDON, Surrey CR9 9EL.

the basic cooking utensils of the Chinese. Small pieces of varied vegetables were frying in it.

The manservant came over and resumed his stirring of the ingredients. 'You would like some?' he suggested. 'I have rice ready.'

'At this time of night?'

'I always wait up for Mr Adams. He likes it if I am here when he comes home.'

'I'm sure he does,' Venetia said drily.

'He is always angry with me because I do not go to bed, and he says he will send me away if I do not obey him. But I know he is pleased to see me.'

As he spoke the man took out a bowl of fluffy white rice from the oven and set it on the kitchen table. He placed the vegetables beside it in another bowl and then added a further dish containing fried prawns and water chestnuts. The smell was tantalising and Venetia accepted a plate and a serving fork. The man—his name was something unpronounceable, so he suggested she call him Yim—had been with Neil for more than ten years.

'I joined Mr Adams when he first came to Hong Kong,' he explained, 'and I have travelled the world with him ever since.'

'You must have been happy that he came back here.'

'Hong Kong is no longer my home. Each time I return there are thousands more Chinese, and old faces are swamped by new ones. I like London. Wardour Street and Soho is all the China I need.'

Venetia laughed and found herself more relaxed than she had been for the whole evening.

'I will get your hot milk,' Yim said.

'Not after prawns and rice. I'll join you with some tea.'

He poured some straw-coloured liquid into a small cup, and as she went to pick it up she heard the sound of a car. She jumped hurriedly to her feet, but the Chinese shook his head. 'It is not Mrs Adams or my master. I know the sound of their car. It is the others.'

'What others?'

'The newspapermen. They began to arrive an hour ago.'

'Newspapermen? Has anything happened? Why are they here?'

'They are waiting to see Mr Adams. They have heard he is having an important meeting tonight and they hope he will give them a statement.'

'I'll be surprised if he does.'

'I have already told them so, but they insist on remaining.'

Venetia went into the hall and peered through a side window. She glimpsed several cars parked outside the gates together with a knot of men, though a few of them had approached to stand by the front steps. Some of them had cameras and they all looked as though they were prepared for a long vigil. Behind her a clock chimed three, and she frowned. Margot had still not returned and when she did, her arrival was bound to cause comment, particularly if she looked the way she had done the last time she had left Boris. Anger at the woman's stupidity and disregard for Neil made Venetia long to shake her. But there was only one thing to do. Hurrying back to her room, she flung on a pair of slacks and a sweater, and raced downstairs again.

Yim was still in the kitchen, and she carefully explained that she wanted to get out of the house without being seen, so that she could try to intercept Boris's car. 'If I wait along the road a couple of hundred yards from the house, I'll see him before he has a chance to come into the driveway.'

'You will bring Mrs Adams back on foot?' the old man ventured.

'No, I'll get into the car *with* her! I want those newshounds outside to think we've all been out together.'

Yim nodded with oriental inscrutability, and moving over to the back door, quietly unlocked it. He advised her to follow the wall until she came to a small door which would bring her on to the roadway a few yards below the main gates.

'If you are careful,' he said, 'you will not be seen. All the newsmen are looking this way. To make more certain I

98

will wait for one minute and then go and stand by the front door. That is sure to attract the attention of the evil ones.'

'Not evil,' she grinned briefly, 'just anxious to do their job.'

Hugging her coat around her, she followed the low wall until she reached the gate. She counted another thirty seconds and then opened it and slipped through. Yim must have done as he had said, for the small crowd of men standing by their cars were all looking in the direction of the house. Tiptoeing carefully to keep her heels off the road, Venetia ran as fast as she could until she reached a bend in it and was out of sight.

Only then did she relax, and slowing her pace, searched for a vantage point from where she could wait for Boris's car. A small light illuminated the gates of another house and seemed to afford her the best position. She waited beside them, stamping her feet against the cold and digging her hands deeply into her pockets. Ten minutes went by and then five more. She flexed her legs and walked up and down to bring back the circulation. The night was stormy, with rain in the air, which clung to her skin and hair. She was not in a position to see the harbour, and she could have been in any dark street in any wealthy residential area.

In the distance there came the drone of a plane, and as it died away she heard another deeper throb. A car engine. Instinctively she knew it was Boris's and she tensed expectantly. If he did not see her by the gate he would go flashing past before she could stop him. Yet to stand in the road would take her away from the light, and in the darkness she ran a serious risk of being mowed down. But determination to protect Neil robbed her of caution and minimised her fear, and as the sound of the engine grew louder still she marched out into the road and waved a white handkerchief. The car drew nearer, its speed unwavering, and she waved her arms and shouted 'Stop!' at the top of her voice, even though she knew she could not be heard.

A cloud scurried away from the moon and faint, watery

rays lit up her pale face. 'Please let Boris see me,' she prayed, as the car came on, and forced herself to remain in its path. The speed of the engine did not waver and she was just poised to fling herself out of the way when brakes squealed, wheels crunched and the bonnet slithered to a stop, its front wing inches from her body.

There was an angry expletive and a window slid down to show Boris's face. 'What the hell are you doing?' he shouted furiously. 'Is this a new way of committing suicide?'

'I had to stop you,' she gasped. 'There was no other way. Where's Margot?'

'Don't tell me you've been waiting here as a watchdog?'

'That's exactly what I've been doing! There are a crowd of photographers outside the house and I don't want them to see you coming back with her alone.'

Boris's expression went blank, then a derisive smile widened his mouth. 'You really are Margot's wet-nurse! I always had my doubts about your being her social secretary. Did Neil hire you from a special agency or were you seconded from Intelligence?'

'I don't know what you're talking about.'

'Oh yes, you do. Adams is scared to death in case his wife's behaviour ruins his work. So he got you out here to keep her in hand. Isn't that so?'

'Where is she?' Venetia insisted.

'See for yourself,' he said, and leaning back in his seat gave her a view of the occupant lying sprawled in the seat beside him.

Venetia stared at the huddle of chiffon and for an instant felt she was looking at a pile of empty clothes, so totally dead to the world was the woman inside them.

'She's ill!' Venetia gasped.

'She's drunk. Get into the car and I'll pull up further along the road.'

She scrambled into the back and the car moved forward and then stopped half in the road and half in someone's drive. The interior reeked of alcohol, and she had to resist the temptation to wind down her window.

'How did it happen?' she asked the man, as he slewed round in his seat to face her.

'We went out for dinner and then returned to my flat. She insisted on having a drink—and the rest you can see for yourself.'

'She doesn't drink,' Venetia said disbelievingly.

Boris gave her a keen look. 'She does when the mood takes her.'

'One drink wouldn't do that,' Venetia pointed to Margot, still dead to the world. 'She looks as if she's knocked back a bottle.'

'She has! I was in the middle of trying to get it away from her when I had a call from New York. I took it in my bedroom and was away for fifteen minutes. When I got back she was dead drunk.' Roughly he shook the thin shoulder and Margot sagged forward in the seat like a puppet with broken strings. 'I tried to get black coffee down her, but it was hopeless, so I let her lie on the settee and hoped she'd sleep it off. At three o'clock I figured it was a waste of time and decided to take her home.'

'You should have phoned me,' Venetia said angrily.

'And run the risk of waking up the whole house?'

'How would you have got her into the house anyway?'

'She has a key in her handbag,' he explained with gentle logic. 'And I know where her bedroom is. I was going to carry her up and leave her there. Then no one would have been any the wiser.'

'Except the whole of Hong Kong,' Venetia said bitterly. 'Can you imagine what would have happened if the photographers had seen you carrying her into the house like that?'

'I wasn't expecting a welcoming committee of photographers,' Boris said patiently. 'If I'd found them there I'd have said she was ill.'

'And reeking of whisky? You must be joking.' Venetia peered over the seat, uncertain what to do, yet knowing she had to do something to save the situation. 'We'd better drive round to the side of the house and try and get in without anyone seeing us.'

'You have to go past the front to get to the side,' Boris explained.

Venetia bit her lip. 'Then we must put her in the back of the car. Help me to get her out.'

'What's all this in aid of?' Boris asked, not moving from his position behind the wheel.

'I've got an idea,' Venetia panted, pulling at Margot's arm. 'Let's hope it comes off.'

'Her arm, or the idea?'

'For heaven's sake!' she flamed. 'Get out and help me, or do you *want* to cause a scandal?'

Boris climbed from the car, pushed Venetia to one side and lifted Margot out. Though no taller than Venetia herself, he had the strength of a gorilla, and held the limp body as though it were made of papier-maché.

'Open the back door,' he said evenly, and carefully deposited Margot on the floor, making sure her head was in contact with the carpet.

'Have you got a rug to put over her?' Venetia asked.

He opened the boot and came back with a soft mound of angora which she draped carefully and completely around Margot, hiding her from sight. Then she took the front seat next to Boris.

'*I'm* your date now,' she said evenly. 'Let's drive to the front of the house, give the photographers a chance to see it isn't Margot, and then head for the side entrance.'

Flinging her an admiring glance, he backed the car on to the road and roared up the incline. As the sound of their engine was heard by the men standing outside the entrance of the Adams' house, they grouped themselves together and blocked the way, making it necessary for Boris to bring the car to a standstill. A couple of enquiring faces peered in and Venetia stared aloofly through the windscreen. There was a flash of bulbs and she blinked and shook her head, then pressed the button for the window to come down.

'Do you mind allowing us to go through to the house?' she said in icy tones.

'We're waiting for Mr Adams,' a man replied. 'We know he's having a secret meeting with the Chinese. When will he be back?'

'I don't know Mr Adams' affairs. I am his wife's secretary.'

'Is Mrs Adams with him?'

'My employer is in her room sleeping, and I would like to be in mine, if you would kindly move out of the way.' Venetia glanced at Boris. '*Drive on,*' she muttered.

He set the car in motion and the cluster of men parted to let them through. As they reached the front door Boris swerved the wheel round and made for the back of the house. Venetia hurriedly glanced through the rear window, but no one was following them and she gave a sigh of relief. If her luck held she might yet be able to save Margot's reputation.

Hardly had the car stopped when the back door opened and Yim shuffled forward. In silence Boris carried Margot inside, with Venetia hurriedly bringing up the rear. At once Yim closed and bolted the door, and Venetia allowed herself a sigh of relief.

'I'll take her to her room,' Boris said, and walked through the hall and up the stairs with the assurance of a man who had done it many times before. He dumped Margot unceremoniously on her bed and looked at Venetia with mocking eyes. 'Margot won't know how to thank you when she wakes up in the morning.'

'I don't want her thanks.'

'You'll get them from Adams. You've saved *him* tonight, did you but know it.'

Had Boris spoken like this earlier today, she would not have understood him, but her last conversation with Neil had made many things clear.

'It's a pity you didn't think of Mr Adams' reputation before you got his wife drunk,' she said steadily.

'My dear girl,' Boris laughed, 'I didn't *need* to get her drunk.' He laughed again. 'She *is* a drunk.'

Venetia felt her scalp prickle, and she stared into the sardonic face. 'You mean she's—she's——'

'An alcoholic,' he said. 'It was naïve of you not to have guessed.'

CHAPTER EIGHT

BORIS's statement kept Venetia awake for the rest of the night. Knowing what was wrong with Margot made many things clear; not least the reason why Neil would not allow his wife to return to England without him. Also clear was his refusal to have any alcohol in the house. With painful clarity she remembered how Margot had taunted him for not serving wine on the evening of her arrival. She had seen this as his desire to instil his own ascetic tastes into others, and writhed with shame that she had misjudged him so badly.

At seven-thirty, with dawn streaking the sky with pink and silver fingers, she went quietly to Margot's room. It had been impossible to undress her last night, and reluctant to call for help at such an hour, she had contented herself with unzipping the black chiffon dress and taking off the silver-strapped shoes.

Margot was still asleep on the bed, covered by the eiderdown which she had placed over her, but though she shook her by the shoulders, Margot did not stir, and deciding to leave her till she awakened normally, Venetia went back to her own room. It was too early to get up and she climbed between the sheets again and closed her eyes.

Surprisingly she fell asleep, and when she awoke it was to bright sun streaming through the window and a pale blue sky flecked with puffball clouds. It was a day to encourage high spirits, yet Venetia's spirits were at their lowest since her arrival here, and she knew they would not revive until she had made her apologies and her peace with Neil Adams.

As she put on a snug-fitting skirt and sweater of sea-green wool that matched the colour of her eyes, she wondered what time he had come in last night—if indeed he had come in at all, and going down in search of breakfast, received her answer from Yim who was on his way up the stairs with a tray. A pot of coffee, half a grapefruit and a silver covered dish from which came the delicious smell of bacon told her it was for Neil.

'Mr Adams is breakfasting late,' she commented.

'He came home an hour ago,' Yim said softly. 'He is very tired.'

Venetia nodded and went on her way, thinking how exhausted Neil must be after such a session. Because of this she was considerably surprised when, crossing from the dining room to the study, she saw him coming down the stairs. As usual he looked dressed for the Foreign Office, in a dark suit and tie and crisp white shirt. His hair gleamed smoothly away from his high forehead, and staring at his pale, glittering eyes—how bright were the yellow flecks in the irises this morning—it was impossible to believe he had been working all night.

'I hope everything went well for you?' she asked.

'As well as I had anticipated. Things obviously went far better with you?'

'I beg your pardon?' The frigidity of his voice dumbfounded her.

'When I left you last night,' he said, 'I was under the impression that you were spending the evening alone. It seems I was wrong.'

'I'm sure that's supposed to mean something,' she replied, 'but I'm afraid I'm in no mood for guessing.'

He reached into the briefcase he was holding and extracted a photograph.

Venetia looked at it. It was a flashlight one and showed the front of the Citroën and a clear picture of Boris and herself. 'I can explain that,' she said quickly.

'Women can always explain everything,' he rasped. 'But I'm not interested in why you were with Kanin. I don't care if you spend all your free time with him, so long as you keep my wife out of trouble.'

'That's exactly what I was doing!'

'By taking Kanin away from her? You don't think Margot will let you get away with that?'

Pushing past her, he strode out of the house. She ran after him, but as she did so she saw the chauffeur by the car, and knowing it was impossible to talk to Neil in front of anyone else, she backed away. She did not blame Neil for jumping to the conclusion he had: the picture he had seen had warranted it. She only regretted that he had not given her the opportunity to explain, though the pleasurable anticipation of being able to make him eat his words was marred by the knowledge that when he did so he would have to admit the truth of Margot's behaviour. Poor Neil. What a fool he was to go on loving someone who cared nothing about him; who went out of her way to hurt him and destroy everything he was working to achieve. The intensity of the anger she felt on his behalf was ridiculous, and not just anger *for* him but *against* him for being so blindly devoted to a woman who did not deserve him.

Margot did not stir from her room all day, and not until late afternoon did she send for Venetia, looking so wan and pale as she greeted her that Venetia's anger withered.

'I suppose Boris brought me back?' Margot enquired, her voice devoid of its usual melodious lilt.

'We both did.'

Briefly Venetia explained what had happened, but Margot paid scant attention and halfway through listening, fell asleep again. Venetia stood looking down at her for several moments, marvelling that there were no signs of dissipation to be seen on the creamy, unlined skin. She remembered that Margot had been confined to her room for a whole day several weeks ago, an attack of migraine, Neil had said at the time, and she wondered now whether this had been a euphemism for yet another lapse on Margot's part. Quietly she crossed to the door and went out.

Her godfather had been wrong to send her here without telling her the whole truth, for that he knew it himself she did not doubt. He had obviously kept silent out of fear that, hearing it, she would refuse to come; yet he must have known that living in the Adams' house she was bound to discover the truth for herself. Perhaps he had hoped that by that time she would be so involved with Neil's affairs, both business and personal, that she would be prepared to see her job through to the end. The old fox was right, of course, she admitted. She would not be able to leave now. Yet anger made her pen a letter to Sir William, and in no uncertain terms she told him how she felt and how she assessed the position.

'I'm living on the edge of a volcano which is likely to erupt any moment. I've done my best to persuade Neil,' she crossed out the Christian name thickly and put 'Mr Adams' above it, 'to allow his wife to return to London, but now I know the truth about her, I can see why he won't let her live on her own. It was wrong of you not to have told me the truth before I came here. No one can control Margot, and it will only be luck if she doesn't destroy herself and her husband too, before his work here is finished.'

Unwilling for the letter to fall into anyone's hands by accident, she went out and posted it herself, taking the opportunity for a brisk stroll down the hillside. It was always easier to descend, and she went further than she had intended, so that by the time she returned home it was an hour later. Neil's car was parked by the front door and she slipped into the hall, intent on making her way to her room before she was seen.

Her foot was on the first stair when he called her name and, heart beating as fast as though she had been caught playing truant, she turned to face him. Again an inexplicable tremor went through her, making her limbs shiver as though with fever. As critically as she could she stared at him, wondering why she should react like this to someone so detached and austere-looking. Not that there was anything austere about him at the moment. His skin—which was normally pale—was flushed pink, and his light brown eyes appeared deeper than usual. Even his voice was different: no longer dry and punctilious but as quick and breathless as her own.

'I want to talk to you, Venetia. Please come here.'

She came abreast of him and he opened the door of the drawing room and inclined his head, so that she was forced to precede him. He closed the door with a sharp click that seemed to indicate it would remain closed until he had said what he intended, and, accepting the inevitability of this, she perched on the edge of a chair and folded her hands in her lap.

'Why did you let me believe what I did?' he began abruptly. 'Why didn't you tell me the truth?'

'I tried to, but you wouldn't listen.'

'Because I was angry.' He ran a hand through his hair, a gesture she had rarely seen him make and one which ruffled its long strands, so that a lock fell forward across his forehead, making him look unexpectedly boyish. 'Yim told me the whole story. You showed great presence of mind—quick thinking.' He gave a deep sigh. 'It was a master-stroke to hide Margot on the floor of the car.'

'It was the only thing I could think of.'

'Kanin must have been furious,' he said.

'Why?'

'Because his plan came unstuck.'

'Unstuck? I don't follow you.'

'You don't think Margot got drunk by accident, do you?' he said drily.

'You're not suggesting Boris did it on purpose?' Venetia could understand Neil's dislike of the man, but was surprised it should lead him to make such an unwarranted assertion.

'That's *exactly* what I'm suggesting,' he reiterated. 'He knows Margot is—that she can't drink—and he deliberately encouraged her to do so. It isn't the first time he's done it, though on the last occasion *I* managed to thwart his plans.' A faint lift of the well-cut mouth was the nearest Neil could come to a smile at this moment. 'He must have been furious that you were on the scene this time.'

'I still don't believe he did it deliberately,' she said flatly. 'Why should he?'

'To discredit me.' Neil went to stand by the mantelpiece and rested his elbow on the shelf. The delicate china objects behind him seemed to be at one with his own fine-cut features, as was their pastel colouring, so subtle yet so unmistakable. 'Two things happened last night: someone tipped off the photographers to be here, and I had a secret meeting with our friends from Peking.'

'You know what secrets are in Hong Kong,' she shrugged.

'Even so, only a handful of people knew about it. Unfortunately one of them was Margot. She was in the library when a call came through for me and she took it.'

'You should instruct the Embassy to be more careful,' Venetia said.

'They don't expect my wife to be a spy,' Neil answered frigidly.

'You're not saying Boris is!'

'Let's say he's not a wellwisher.'

'But what does he have to gain? I could understand it if it were Simon.'

'Simon Hoy is a clever businessman. If he can't make money one way he has sufficient confidence in himself to know he'll make it in another. He, and other people like him, might not want our talks to succeed but they wouldn't actively do anything to scuttle them. Kanin is in a different category. He's a Russian, don't forget.'

'His parents were,' she amended, 'and they ran away during the Revolution.'

'Kanin lived in Moscow from the time he was sixteen to twenty-four.' The answer was positive and not to be denied. 'Formative years for anyone, Venetia, particularly for a man of his temperament.'

'But why should the Russians care about your talks with the Chinese? It's only a trade pact.'

'It will stabilise China's position in the world, and that's something our Russian friends don't want.'

Though she was prepared to accept the validity of this remark, she could not accept the part Neil had assigned to Boris.

'Are you suggesting it was *Boris* who tipped off the photographers to come here?' she asked slowly.

'Yes. Somebody made an anonymous call to the newspaper office and told them I was attending a secret meeting. Kanin planned to bring Margot home drunk at three o'clock in the morning, which would have made a very good picture for the front page of the *Hong Kong News*.'

'And you would have lost face.'

'Do you still doubt the importance of that?'

'No,' she said slowly. 'You made that point very clear to me last night and I accept it.'

'But you won't accept my statement about Boris?'

'Let's say I find it difficult.' She suddenly remembered the photograph of herself and Boris, and asked him where he had got it.

'Another wellwisher,' he said wryly, 'but a genuine one this time. It's a reporter who works on the city desk. The editor was all set to use it when my friend pointed out that the picture was not of my wife, but of my wife's secretary.' Neil Adams straightened from the fireplace and put his hands in the pockets of his jacket. 'I appreciate what you did—spoiling your own name in order to protect Margot's and mine.'

'I was protecting the success of your work, not your good name!'

His slight smile showed that he took the point. 'Even so, I appreciate the gesture. Despite these permissive times one doesn't lightly throw away one's reputation.'

'I don't think a girl's reputation is lost by coming home at three o'clock in the morning with a man,' Venetia said crisply. 'If I'd been to *his* home it might have been different.'

'You don't like being thanked, do you?' he said mildly.

'Not when it isn't necessary.' She stood up. 'Anyway, I owe you an apology for what I said to you last night—and even before that. About you not letting your wife return to England without you ... I wouldn't have said it if I had known the truth.'

Blue shadowed lids hid the brown eyes. 'You mean Sir William didn't tell you?' Then, as she shook her head, he gave a sigh of exasperation. 'No wonder you thought I was crazy!'

'Not crazy. Just that you loved your wife obsessively.'

'And now?' The question was a mere thread of sound, but the insistent way he was looking at her told her he expected an answer.

'Now I see it as a desire to protect her.' Venetia blinked away her tears. 'I hope Margot appreciates how much you love her.'

'I'm not concerned with her appreciation,' he said bleakly.

He walked over to the sideboard and she watched him. No, Neil Adams was not the type of man to worry if his gestures were appreciated, nor if his love was requited. Once he had given it, it would remain given.

'I think we deserve a drink.' His voice broke into her thoughts and without waiting for her to reply he opened a section of the panelled wall and inserted a key in an almost invisible lock. A door swung back to disclose several bottles. He took one out and poured two sherries, handed her one and then carefully went back and locked the cupboard. 'Practice makes perfect,' he said, interpreting her look. 'I've had five years of it.'

'Margot didn't drink before?'

'Not so badly that it was an illness. It *is* an illness, you know. She knows it's destroying her, but she can't stop.'

'She has everything,' Venetia whispered. 'Beauty, intelligence, money. Why does she want to destroy herself?'

'She wants to destroy *me*,' he corrected, and raised his glass. 'Let's drink to the future, Venetia. It has to be better than the past!'

Venetia accepted the toast, knowing this was his way of telling her he had no intention of explaining the first part of his remark.

Margot did not come down to dinner and Venetia dined

alone with Neil. It was strange to sit opposite him in the dining room and she made an effort to forget all she had learned today. But it was impossible to put it out of her mind, particularly since it gave her a new understanding of him. For his part Neil seemed in a more talkative mood, and as if sensing she wanted to forget the events of the night before, he entertained her with stories of his previous posts, many of which had taken him to other countries.

'I hadn't realised you were a full-time diplomat,' she remarked after he had recounted a particularly hair-raising story of a six-month sojourn in Chile.

'I see myself as more of a trouble-shooter,' he corrected.

'I can't see you as a muscle-man!'

'I used to box,' he murmured.

'With great attention to Queensberry rules, I'm sure!'

'A few punches below the belt, too. I was expelled from Eton for hitting a master.'

'I don't believe it.'

'It's true.' He offered her a selection from a bowl of fruit. 'He set about a friend of mine in a particularly vicious way and I vowed to get him for it. I did eventually, and got myself thrown out.'

She tried, and failed, to imagine him plotting anyone's downfall, and was so curious to know exactly what he had done that she asked him.

'I took lessons in Judo for a year and then gave him a thrashing.'

'That's just the sort of thing I can imagine you doing,' she gurgled. 'Other boys would have rushed in, arms flailing, but you bided your time for a year and then went in for the kill.'

'How unpleasant you make it sound!'

'It was very civilised,' she retorted, waving a half-cut peach in the air, and only realised she was doing it as she saw him glance at her hand. 'I've drunk too much wine,' she said. 'You shouldn't have given me the second glass.'

'We both deserved to relax tonight. But you're not drunk with wine, Venetia, only with tiredness.'

'You must be tired too. You didn't get any sleep either.'

'I can catnap. A ten-minute doze and I'm as good as new.'

'How perfect you are! I don't mean that sarcastically,' she added as he shot her a quizzical glance. 'But you're so self-contained. Everything you do is always right.'

'Not always.'

'I'm sure it is,' she persisted. 'I can't imagine you doing anything to hurt anyone.'

'If only that were true!' The words seemed pulled from him, and he abruptly pushed back his chair and stood up.

Concerned that she had said something to upset him, though she did not know what it could be, she remained in her chair looking at his back, and after a moment he gained control of himself and returned to the table. 'Forgive me, Venetia, perhaps I'm tired after all. I don't usually lose control like that.'

'It might be better for you if you did.'

'No.' It was a sound of pure agony, as though wrenched from the very depths of his being. But this time he made no effort to regain his equilibrium, and pushing back his chair again, strode from the room.

Appalled by the suffering she had seen on his face, she hurried after him, but the door leading to the library was closed, and realising he did not wish to see her, she returned to the dining room. The half-eaten peach, so sweet a moment ago, now tasted like acid, and crumpling her napkin, she went to her room. For her too, the day had gone on long enough.

CHAPTER NINE

VENETIA was still asleep the next morning when Margot came to her room. But what a different Margot she was from the day before! Looking at the radiant face and sparkling eyes, the quick vivacious movements as she drifted round the room, Venetia found it impossible to believe that twenty-four hours ago she had been slumped in a drunken coma.

'Boris tells me I owe you my reputation,' she said the moment Venetia opened her eyes. 'I knew I could trust you the moment I saw you.'

'Don't try that trust too far.' Venetia sat up in bed and pulled the sheet around her shoulders. Because of the central heating she kept the window open, and a cold breeze was blowing into the room. But Margot did not appear to notice it and was sitting in a chair by the side of the bed. 'You must let me buy you something: a dress perhaps, or a piece of jewellery.'

'I don't need thanks for what I did. It's part of the job.'

'Were you surprised?' Margot asked, and there was a sudden sly look on her face that robbed it of beauty.

As always Venetia was disconcerted that Margot's looks could alter so quickly. Perhaps it was because they came solely from her appearance, rather than from within—or perhaps I'm just being catty, Venetia decided, and pushed both thoughts away.

'Have you had treatment for your drinking?' she asked carefully.

'I'm not ill and I don't need treatment. I drink because it helps me to forget.' Margot jumped up and went to stand by the window. Her delicate profile was serious, though there was a glazed look in her eyes that told Venetia she was seeing nothing.

Was she drinking to forget? And was drink the only solution? Although her curiosity was intense, Venetia was afraid that if they continued this conversation it would arouse memories that would send this beautiful redheaded woman in yet another search for oblivion.

'I forgot to tell you I had a call from the Chairman of the Orphanage yesterday,' she said brightly. 'A Mrs Bloxton. She wants to know if you'll reconsider your decision about taking her place.'

'She knows damn well I won't!' The words were almost spat across the room. 'It's a good thing she didn't get *me* on the other end of the line, or I'd have given her a piece of my mind. An orphanage is the last thing in the world I want to be bothered with.'

'Don't you like children?'

'Like them?' Margot threw back her head and laughed. 'Don't I *like* them?' She laughed again, the sound rising high and clear as peal after peal shook her slender frame.

Frightened she might be going into hysteria, Venetia jumped out of bed and ran over to her. 'I didn't mean to upset you. Can I get you anything? Margot, what have I said?'

'You don't know, do you?' With a visible effort the woman regained control of herself, but she was still trembling violently and she clutched at Venetia and moved over to sit on the bed. 'I thought Neil had told you, but perhaps he can't bear to talk of it either ... any more than I can.'

'Then don't talk about it,' Venetia said urgently, disturbed by the waxen pallor of Margot's skin. 'I'll have a bath and dress, and we can go into town. You said you'd like to—to buy me a dress, but you can buy me a scarf instead. It's so windy here I can do with——'

'I can never have children,' Margot interrupted in a bright, conversational voice.

Venetia's prattle died in her throat and for a second she was unable to speak. 'I'm sorry. I didn't know.'

'It isn't something one talks about. I wanted children desperately—I could have given them so much ... the world would have been their——' The heavy lids lowered, and as they hid the deep blue irises the face became a mask. 'If it hadn't been for Neil ... I'll never forgive him. Never!'

The silence lengthened and Margot remained on the bed as though in a trance, her hands clasped in her lap, her head half thrown back to show the long white throat, graceful as that of a swan.

'I'm sure Neil is upset about it too,' Venetia said gently, uttering the first words that came into her head in the hope of bringing Margot back to the present.

But hardly had she spoken when the lids lifted and the blue eyes stared at her, almost black with the hatred that seeped out from within.

'Of course he's upset about it! It's *his* fault I can never have children. If it hadn't been for him ...' The red head tilted and a shaft of sunlight from the window turned it into a crown of flame. 'He killed our baby!' she cried. 'It would have been five years old this week. Five years, Venetia. Five years of knowing that for the rest of your life you will be an empty shell, like a tree that can bear no fruit. Do you know what it's like to ache for a baby and never be able to have one?'

'I think so,' Venetia answered quietly. 'But there are many couples who——'

'I'm not talking about couples who can't have children for physical reasons,' Margot cut in angrily. 'I'm talking of someone who *could* have had a child if it hadn't been for her husband's reckless stupidity!'

Hurriedly Venetia went to the wardrobe and made a pretence of choosing a dress. It was difficult because her hands were shaking, but she resolutely continued to fumble among the clothes. The last thing in the world she wanted was for Margot to confide in her, for then she would be forced into replying.

'Haven't you ever wondered why he won't let me out of his sight?' Margot was still speaking. 'It isn't only because I drink that he's scared of leaving me alone—if it was just that he'd have let me drink myself to death years ago—then he'd be rid of me! It's because he feels guilty. That's why he has to protect me!'

'He loves you!' Venetia swung round. 'How can you doubt it? He loves you and he wants to help you.'

'He hates me and he wants me to die! Then his guilt will die too.'

The brutal words fell like heavy stones in a pool, rippling out and encompassing Venetia in horror. 'Why should he feel guilty?'

'Because he was driving the car when we crashed. Driving like a maniac! I was in hospital for three months and my baby was born dead.'

'Oh, Margot.' Venetia took a step forward, but the thin figure gave a disclamatory movement.

'It's over and done with. But now you know why I hate him. Why I'll go on hating him for the rest of my life!'

'But can't you——'

'And that's why he won't leave me,' Margot added. 'No matter what I do to him, he'll never go away!'

'He stays because he loves you,' Venetia reiterated.

'He stays because he also blames himself for my drinking.' The blue eyes were mocking. 'I only started to do so after the accident. So you see he has a lot to feel guilty for!'

'Is that why you do it? Because you know it hurts *him* as well as yourself?'

'Maybe. I hadn't thought of it that way. I started drinking to help me forget and then it became something I couldn't control.'

'You do control it, though.'

'Because Neil watches me like a hawk. Even when I go out there's always one of his people around. That's why I was so sure he'd told you the truth. I still can't believe he didn't.'

'He didn't,' Venetia said firmly. 'Perhaps he's hoping you're getting better.'

'When pigs can fly!' Margot said rudely. 'You do live in

118

fairyland, don't you? Still, it's better than living in my kind of hell.'

'It's a hell of your own making.'

'Spare me the psychology! At least till you've had some suffering of your own!' The full skirts rustled angrily round Margot's narrow, arched feet, but when she spoke again her voice was bright. 'I'm going to my dressmaker for a fitting. Come with me. I'll meet you downstairs in half an hour.'

At eleven they left the house and drove down to Victoria Harbour and across to Kowloon, finally stopping outside a small building behind the Penninsula Hotel.

'I was told dressmakers come and fit you in your own home,' Venetia murmured, as they went up in an elevator to the top floor.

'So they do, but I like to get out of the house. Anyway, if I come here I can see all the materials she has. I always plan on buying one thing and end up with ten. Are you sure you won't let me buy you a dress?'

'I don't need payment for what I did last night.'

'Neil thinks you do. After all, you saved *his* face! Mine doesn't matter.' Seeing Venetia's surprise, she gave a wide smile. 'I couldn't care less what people say about *me*. The more they gossip the more I love it.'

'But why?'

'Because then they gossip about Neil too. And that's what I want—to make him a laughing-stock!'

For the second time this morning Venetia was aghast at what she had heard. 'How can you talk like that about your husband?'

'He killed my baby!'

'It was his child too.'

'It was *my* child. I was carrying it. What did it mean to him? What does any child mean to a man until it's born? But to a woman it means everything.'

The automatic gates parted and Margot readjusted her expression and stepped into the showroom. At once two young Chinese girls descended on her and ushered her towards a middle-aged woman of European descent.

With an effort Venetia tried to pay attention to what was going on, but she was still confused by Margot's last bitter words, for they indicated not only anger against Neil, but a lethal hatred that could well destroy him.

She tried to dismiss the idea as ridiculous, but it would not disappear, and all she could think of was Neil's own words regarding loss of face and the importance of maintaining it when dealing with the Chinese. Margot obviously knew how important it was for him to merit no gossip or scandal, yet she had said she would willingly do anything to destroy him, even if she had to destroy herself in the process. And what better way of doing this than by cuckolding him? Even in Western society it would make him a laughable object. How much more so in a society whose roots were still firmly entrenched in a past where man was lord and master?

But surely when it came to it, Margot would not deliberately ruin her own name and reputation in order to ruin her husband's? But events showed all too clearly that this was exactly what she would do, and Venetia knew, with deep certainty, that Margot's liking for Boris was fanned by her desire to harm Neil. Even her drinking bouts were her way of making him pay for causing the death of their unborn child.

The death of a child. The words fell around Venetia like a shroud. It was impossible to believe Neil could have driven so recklessly as to have caused an accident. Her brows drew together as she tried to remember Margot's exact words. But even if she could recall them they would still not tell her the true story: that would only come from hearing Neil's side of it. Somehow she could not envisage him talking of something that affected him so deeply, for that it did affect him she had no doubt. It explained his entire behaviour towards his wife: his quiet acceptance of her moods and tantrums. And of her men, too. Venetia sighed. How deeply he must love her to be capable of such guilt and such a sacrifice of his own manhood.

'Do you like this dress?' Margot's question brought Venetia back to the room and the crowd of smiling Chinese girls, presided over by the dumpy figure of the French dressmaker.

The dress in question was the loveliest Venetia had seen. Unlike so many made in Hong Kong, it was devoid of beading and relied for its appeal on superb cut and material. A deceptively simple bodice gave way to a long full skirt that remained sleek as its owner stood still, but fanned out into a circle at the slightest movement. Movement also drew attention to the richness of the oyster satin which, under the light, gleamed with the pink iridescence of a pearl.

'You look beautiful in it,' Venetia said truthfully.

'It is your style too,' the dressmaker said, her dark eyes appraising Venetia's dramatic colouring and slenderness. 'You would not want exactly the same as Mrs Adams, but I have a very similar——'

'No, thank you,' Venetia said hastily. 'I'm here as Mrs Adams' secretary, not a potential client!'

'Secretaries wear clothes too. When you first came in I thought you and Mrs Adams were sisters.'

Embarrassed, Venetia glanced quickly round, but Margot seemed delighted by the remark and laughed gaily. 'It's because we're both slim and tall. But our colouring's quite different, Mrs Dubrofsky.'

'You are the negative and the positive,' the dressmaker said gutturally.

'I'm obviously the negative one,' Venetia smiled, and touched her black hair.

'I do not mean it as an insult.' Mrs Dubrofsky went closer to Venetia. 'There are great possibilities in a negative. It can be well developed, for instance, and developed in many different ways too.'

At this Venetia laughed. 'You make me sound as if I'm under-developed!'

'A little, perhaps,' the dressmaker agreed. 'You need stronger chemicals, eh?'

'The chemical attraction of a man is all my secretary needs,' Margot intervened, moving to the changing-room. 'That would develop her in every possible way!'

The comment was lightly made, but Venetia could not help wondering if there was a hidden meaning behind it. Somehow she did not think so. Until this morning she and Margot had never exchanged confidences, if exchanged was the right word to use, for the woman was so involved with her own affairs—both unhappy past ones and the pleasurable ones of the moment—that she was totally unconcerned for anyone else's feelings. In that sense she was a supreme egoist, believing that not only did the world revolve around her, but that she was indeed the world.

It was after one o'clock when they returned to the island of Hong Kong, and as they emerged from the tunnel Margot looked artlessly at Venetia.

'You can take the afternoon off, if you like. I won't be needing you. I'm meeting Boris.'

'Is that wise?' The question slipped out, and seeing the full lips tighten, she knew she should have kept quiet.

'I'll let you know when I want your opinion!' snapped Margot.

'I'm sorry. I just thought——'

'You're not being paid to think—just to keep me company.'

'You're not giving me much opportunity to do that. You seem more intent on getting rid of me.'

'I'd like to get rid of you permanently, and Neil too!'

Surprised by the unexpected attack, Venetia fell silent. The car purred on, the chauffeur shielded from them by a glass partition so that she had the feeling she was cocooned from the world. But even in a cocoon one could be hurt, as she was hurt now, not only by what Margot had said, but by something indefinable which, through her very inability to pinpoint it, was all the more worrying. Why was she so sensitive and edgy? Why should she feel as if life was passing her by? Could Margot, with her flamboyant beauty and the devotion of two men, be making her realise how dull her own life was? Yet this was not true; she had a host of friends in London and had turned down several offers of marriage. Even in Hong Kong she had Simon, who was making no secret of his attraction for her.

'Forgive me, Venetia.' Margot was speaking again, contrite as she always was when she had lost her temper. 'I didn't mean what I said. I'm just in a bad mood and angry with Neil for spoiling my life.'

'You're spoiling his as well!' Venetia's bluntness was deliberate, but then one could not be on the receiving end all the time. At least she couldn't.

If Margot was surprised by the retort she did not show it, but settled back again in her seat, content now that she had made her apology to sit in silence until they reached the Mandarin Hotel.

'Do you mind getting out here, Venetia? I'm sure you'll enjoy looking round the shops, and if you see that scarf you wanted, be a darling and buy it for yourself.'

'Thanks.' Venetia stepped on to the pavement. 'What time do you want me home?'

'I don't care. I'll probably be dining with Boris.' The eyes grew a deeper blue as malice darkened them. 'I won't come home drunk tonight, so you needn't wait up for me.'

'How can you be sure?'

'One can never be sure of anything in this life! Let's just say I feel it in my bones.'

Dispiritedly Venetia went into the hotel. The lobby was full of people and she went into the lounge, past the immense mural on the wall—its colours so delicate that one could almost pass it by without seeing it—and up to the mezzanine floor where waiters were busy dispensing coffee. The smell of it decided her she was too hungry for a snack, and finding the idea of lunching alone in the restaurant unappealing, she went down the stairs in the direction of the Coffee Shop. On the bottom step she paused for a closer look at the mural, wondering why it did not appeal to her.

123

Perhaps she found its delicacy of colour too negative. The words reminded her of Mrs Dubrofsky and she put her hand to her hair.

'It looks lovely as it is. Don't touch it.' The quiet voice behind her brought her hand to a standstill, and slowly she turned to see Neil Adams. He was so close that their shoulders were almost touching, and she noticed the fine lines fanning out from his eyes.

'I didn't expect to find you here, Venetia. Is Margot with you?'

Venetia coloured, and his mouth, which had softened as he looked at her, grew hard again. 'Boris?' he said, and at her nod, frowned. 'Couldn't you have insisted on going with her?'

'Not short of having a fight on the steps of the hotel. I didn't think you'd take very kindly to that.'

'Spare me the sarcasm!'

'Then spare me the naïveté!' For the second time today her tongue had run away with her, and colour flooded into her face. 'I'm sorry, I shouldn't have said that. I don't know what's come over me this morning.'

'Too many problems with Mr and Mrs Adams,' he said with unexpected bitterness. 'I'm not surprised you're irritable. Forgive me.'

'That's the second time I've been asked to do that. Margot said it too.'

'She has less to be forgiven for than I have.' Abruptly he swung round and stared at the mural, and Venetia, understanding what his words meant, looked at him with sympathy.

Unexpectedly he turned and caught her off guard, and their gaze met and held. Even in high heels she had to tilt her head back to look at him. It was not something she was used to doing, though she was unaware of having given her thoughts away until he said: 'I'm six feet three inches. Even *you* have to look up to me!'

'Only because of your height,' she said coolly. 'I don't believe in women looking up to men.'

'I don't blame you.' He rubbed his tongue over his lower lip. 'If you were dropped here unexpectedly, I take it you're free for lunch?'

'Yes, but——'

'Then perhaps you'll lunch with me?'

'But——'

'I've never heard so many "buts" in my life!' He seemed suddenly to be in good humour, for not giving her a chance to say any more, he caught her elbow and guided her through the lobby to the elevators.

His fingers were firm through the thin material of her jacket and she was conscious that they remained there as they entered the lift and went up to the Grill Room.

'I assume you've already seen the view from the restaurant on the top floor?' he asked.

'Yes, I have. How did you know?'

'Because Mr Hoy has already taken you here to lunch, and the roof-top restaurant is the obvious choice.'

'You make it sound as if it wouldn't have been yours.'

'I try not to be obvious.'

'I don't think you'd need to try.'

His eyes narrowed. 'I sense you mean that as a compliment, but I can't quite see it!'

She laughed. 'I believe you'd be different without having to think about it.'

He looked pleased, though when next he spoke it was to change the conversation entirely. For the next hour they talked of London and Sir William, and his own discussions with the Chinese. Neil was more forthcoming about them than she had expected, and aware of her surprise he said: 'I had a letter from Sir William this morning. He sends you his love, by the way, and devoted a paragraph in praise of you.'

'He must have an even more difficult job lined up for me when I get back!'

'Even more difficult?'

Venetia lowered her eyes and wished she could kick herself. 'I'm about as diplomatic as a——'

'Don't apologise. Your unguarded tongue at least shows you are relaxed with me.'

'Now that *was* diplomatic!'

He chuckled. 'As I was saying, Sir William extolled your virtues at considerable length. One of them, he said, is discretion. I suppose that's why I'm talking to you like this. Sometimes it's hard not to be able to discuss one's problems with someone else.'

'What about the men who work with you?'

'I don't like them to know my doubts—or even that I have any.'

'I didn't think you did doubt the ultimate success of your talks.'

'One can never tell with the Chinese.'

'I thought your dinner the other night was a success?'

'It was. I'm giving another one in a couple of days.' He leaned on the table. 'At my home.'

'Not the Embassy?'

'It can't be there. It's an unofficial meeting. I was talking to Mao Yeng—the leader of the Chinese delegation—about antique furniture and mentioned I'd shipped out some of my own. He said he'd like to see it. Margot doesn't know yet, but she'll have to act as hostess.'

Remembering Margot's many unflattering remarks about the Chinese, Venetia doubted the wisdom of this, and again the man opposite read her thoughts.

'I'm relying on you to persuade her to play the hostess with charm and tact.'

'You're the best person to do that.'

His laugh was short. 'Knowing I want her to do it will make her do the exact opposite. Surely you know that by now?'

'I—er——'

'Don't pretend, Venetia. You make such a point of honesty.'

Resolutely she said nothing. If she spoke it would only be to ask how he could bear to continue living with someone who did not want him. No matter how guilty he felt over the accident and the loss of the baby, how could he go on expiating it for the rest of his life? She pushed the question aside: not only because she had no right to ask it, but because she knew she would not like the answer she would get if she did so.

'Care for a drive?' he asked.

'I don't want to bother you. I can easily get a taxi back.'

'I wasn't suggesting taking you home. I thought you might care for a trip to the New Territories, unless you've already seen them?'

'No, I haven't. But don't you have work to do?'

'I've decided to play truant if you'll agree to let me take you out.'

She had never expected to hear him ask for her company and she was warmed by it. It was a warmth that remained with her as they went down to his car, though a little of it evaporated as she saw the chauffeur at the wheel and remembered why Neil would never drive again.

Once more she crossed to Kowloon and drove down the long main road—busy as Regent Street—and out past the high-rise blocks of apartment houses built by the Government to accommodate the thousands of Chinese whose numbers were swollen each year by the entry of illegal immigrants. But once past the city and the suburbs, and through the Lion Rock tunnel, she was struck by the comparative emptiness of the countryside, with its green fields, rice paddies and innumerable duck farms.

'The beginning of Peking Duck!' Neil told her, pointing a long finger down into a valley where several women, up to their knees in water, were moving through row upon row of these waterfowl.

'I'll remember that when I eat some!' she smiled.

'They do it excellently at the Mandarin. I'll take you there again one evening.'

She was surprised by the pleasure she felt at his remark, and she looked around her with even happier eyes, charmed by the water buffalo who slowly and calmly pulled ancient ploughs over sharply contoured fields, many carrying water on a yoke across their backs, and rhythmically moving from side to side to let it spray out over the growing vegetables, while stooping in the paddyfields up to their knees in water, women were busy among the bright green shoots.

Along the shoreline on her left she glimpsed innumerable sampans, some moving out to sea to fish, and others returning, while an occasional large junk, its sails billowing in the breeze, gracefully weaved its way between them.

'I wish I'd brought my camera,' she mourned. 'I'll never be able to describe it.'

'There's an even better view to come,' he told her.

'Where?'

'On the Chinese border! We'll be there in another twenty minutes.'

Contentedly she sat and watched the passing scene. Apart from the fields and duck farms, there were many magnificent Chinese-style homes, where wealthy Chinese lived and commuted daily to Kowloon or Victoria. There were also several squalid villages: shacks built into the hillsides or whole fishing communities living on boats along the shore, each junk so closely moored to its neighbour that one could walk from one end of the community to the other without needing to set foot on the ground.

'We're nearly at the border,' Neil murmured as the car swung sharp right and up a very steep road, coming to a stop before a line of stalls. Here, silk coolie hats, beads and various other trivia were displayed to attract the tourists, of whom a great many were milling around, exclaiming excitedly in Japanese, American, French and a preponderance of German.

Instructing the chauffeur to wait, Neil led her past the stalls and up the hill to the highest vantage point. A circle of exquisitely shaped trees lay before them, and beyond it stretched a beige and barren plain.

'China,' he said quietly. 'The reason why you came to Hong Kong.'

Venetia stared at the landscape—disappointed that it

was so drab and mundane, so lacking in form and colour. She half turned away and saw that Neil was gazing at it spellbound. Feeling like a hedonist, she turned to look at the plain once more, and concentrating carefully, began to distinguish objects. It was far from being as deserted as she had thought, and she was able to make out an occasional watch-tower and village. But even so it was difficult to believe she was looking at a land of nine hundred million people.

'Disappointed?' Neil asked.

'A bit,' she said candidly. 'I was expecting something to hit me in the eye.'

'That wouldn't be very Chinese! They are much more subtle than that—even in their scenery. Look at the colours of it.' He gripped her hand to turn her, and she hastily stared down the hillside. 'See all those different shades of green and the soft browns that almost merge into them, but don't quite? Look at the trees too, they're in full leaf, but you can see every line of the branch. It's like a living piece of lacework.'

Carefully she looked, seeing the land take shape and form in front of her. 'You should have been a writer, Neil. You've made the whole view come alive.'

'Do you still find it dull?' he asked.

'Oh, no. It's beautiful. Tranquil and beautiful.'

'Like you.'

Taken by surprise, she remained motionless, letting the words drift around her like petals, afraid that if she moved they would float away as if they had never been said.

'Does it surprise you to know that I see you like a Chinese landscape?' he asked softly.

'Tall and gangling with branches showing!' she said, pulling away from his hand.

'Subtle and delicate,' he corrected, 'and at first glance giving no indication of all the beautiful colours.'

'Madame Dubrofsky called me a negative film,' she said.

'Then I commend her discernment. You *are* a negative—

with all the potential waiting to be developed.'

'If I didn't know you better,' she said lightly, 'I'd say you were flirting with me.'

'You don't know me at all,' he replied.

'Can one person ever really know another one?' She kept the question impersonal, and deliberately moved away from him to stand beside one of the trees.

A group of tourists had already been and gone, and for the moment they were alone up here, with hundreds of miles of land around them and no one to hear what they were saying. It made her feel as alone with him as if they were on a desert island, and she was intensely aware of his nearness and tallness, and the fact that he was no longer looking at her with his usual detached calm, but with a smile on his mouth and a light in his eyes that she had never seen before.

'You could accidentally trip and fall into my arms,' he said, coming purposefully towards her. 'Or I could move and pretend to knock into you. But I don't think either of us are good at the game of pretending.'

'You should be,' she reminded him. 'You're a diplomat.'

'I'm not a diplomat with you,' he said unevenly. 'I'm very much a man. Quite how much I never knew till now.'

With a violence that could never be called detached, he pulled her close and there was no calm in the hard pressure of his mouth, no coldness in the heat of his kiss. It was a heat that enveloped her and scorched her, and though she tried to draw away from him she was powerless to move, for his hands were firm beneath her jacket, holding her close through the thin silk of her blouse and pressing her body tightly against his so that she could feel its trembling.

Determined not to respond to him, she opened her eyes. She glimpsed closed lids, a fine line of eyebrow and soft fair hair, its texture like spun silk. With a gasp she went to push him away, but though Neil lifted his mouth away from hers, he did not let her go. His eyes were now open too, the pupils dilated and making the eyes themselves seem larger and darker. There was a tenderness in them she had never seen before, as there was a tenderness in the thin contours of his face. The tension had gone from it and his features were relaxed and soft. It took years from his age and she was suddenly able to visualise him as a child, thin and pale, yet somehow very intense and vulnerable because of it. As he was so very vulnerable now.

Without another word he started to kiss her again, and this time she responded to him, twining her arms around his neck and running her fingers through his hair. This kiss was different from the first, for the hardness was gone and the passion was fired by tenderness. His hands moved along her spine and down her hips, and she shivered and pressed closer to him, marvelling that he could be so tall and thin, and yet so rightly shaped that they fitted curve into curve, bone into bone. Time stood still as they remained locked in each other's arms, and it was only the harsh sound of a motor-bike in the distance that made them finally draw apart.

Shy of looking at him, she averted her head. Her thoughts were chaotic and since none of them made sense, she remained silent, clenching her hands as she waited for her heartbeats to slow down and her body to stop shaking, knowing that until it did she would not be able to walk a step. Through her lashes she glanced at Neil. He looked as imperturbable as ever, only the faint flush on his skin giving any indication of his earlier passion. Not quite the only indication, she amended, for his mouth was still soft, the lower lip trembling slightly.

'Forgive me, Venetia. I'm sorry for what happened, but I—I've always found this view moving. It must have affected me more today than—than I'd realised.'

His calm words were so unexpected that she was shaken. She had anticipated an apology, perhaps even a defence, but not this matter-of-fact explanation.

'Perhaps I was standing in for China,' she said drily.

'I beg your pardon?'

'You were seeing how far you could go,' she explained, and was pleased to see his flush deepen to red.

'I wouldn't want to see how far I could go with you, Venetia.'

'Because you might fail, or might succeed?'

'Either would be unbearable. If I failed I'd want to keep on trying until I had succeeded, and if I succeeded it would be impossible for me to stop.' The tightness with which he caught her hand belied the coolness of his voice. 'And we *have* to stop. You know that without my telling you. There's Margot.'

'Whom you love,' she said gently, marvelling that she had the willpower to say the words. 'I know she tries your patience and your nerves, and because of it you need an outlet.'

'You're not an outlet!' he said savagely. 'What happened just now was an accident. I give you my word it will never happen again. But somehow this afternoon—with you beside me ... I couldn't take the isolation any more.'

'I understand.' She started to walk in the direction of the car and he kept in step with her. The purely physical movement helped her to keep control of herself, and she was able to look unconcerned as they reached the car and climbed into the back.

Only as they drove down the hill did she allow herself to relax a little. How cautiously Neil had put his thoughts into words, yet how clearly she knew what he meant. He could no longer bear the isolation. What an old-fashioned word, but how aptly it described his position; the isolation of loving a woman who did not want him; of desiring a body he could not touch. No wonder he had turned to the first girl he had felt able to trust. Sir William's avowal of her discretion had served its purpose in a way he had never envisaged.

Tears blurred her eyes and she wiped them away. With a suddenness that was almost her undoing, his hand came out and gripped hers.

'Don't cry over me,' he said tightly. 'I have enough on

my conscience without having your tears as well.'

She turned in her seat to look at him, but he continued to stare straight ahead.

'Don't say anything,' he said tensely. 'Not a word.'

Silently she withdrew her hands and clasped them together on her lap. He was right. Words were not necessary. Indeed no words were needed to make her understand her feelings. All at once the reason for her dejection, for her sudden moods of elation and depression were all too clear. Anger had first made her aware of Neil Adams. Then had come contempt for his weakness, and finally pity for his predicament. But when had pity become love? For that it was love she had no doubt; nor did she doubt that her love had no future. He was tied to Margot, not only by his present commitments, but by past ones, and the past could never be obliterated.

CHAPTER TEN

VENETIA's one desire was to hide. To be alone to think about the love she had just discovered, almost as though she hoped that thinking about it logically would help her to analyse it away. But she dared not think about Neil while he was sitting quietly beside her, his body so relaxed that it was hard to believe that only a short while ago he had been overcome by a passion as deep as her own. Deeper in fact, for it was his intensity that had aroused hers.

How carefree she had been this time a month ago! Then she had not even known that Neil and Margot Adams existed. But now they were a part of her life, and unhappily, a part of her future, for even when she returned to England and their paths no longer crossed, memory of Neil would provide a constant comparison with any other man she met, spoiling her for marriage with anyone else but the one man who would never be free to make her his wife.

It was incredible she should feel this way about someone she hardly knew. Careful to keep her body motionless, she half turned her head, unwilling to let him know she was looking at him. But she might just as well have swivelled round completely, so oblivious was he to his surroundings. Whatever unhappiness he was causing her, his own was even worse, for there were new lines on his face and his pale skin was robbed of its last vestige of colour. Yet nothing could detract from the fine-cut features and precise modelling of his bones. As an old man Neil would be distinguished and patrician, and as a young one—albeit a deeply unhappy one—he had the power to turn over her heart.

'I hope you aren't going to ask me if you can leave Hong Kong?' His voice was unusually loud in the quietness of the car, though it was what he said, rather than the way he said it, that shocked her.

'You mean you wouldn't let me leave?'

'I'm not sure. But I'm hoping you won't ask me. I—er—we still need you.'

' "We" being Queen and Country?' she said sarcastically.

'Naturally. You knew *that* when Sir William asked you to come here.'

'There were a lot of things I *didn't* know,' she said tightly. 'You can't expect me to remain here. Not now.'

'Because of a kiss?' The carelessness in his words was at variance with the rigid way he was holding himself, and gave away his uncertainty.

'Not just *any* kiss,' she retorted, 'but a kiss from the man you're working for. That makes it embarrassing.'

'It needn't be. I've already promised you it won't happen again.'

This was not what she wanted to hear, but at least it saved her pride, for it showed he had no idea how she felt about him. But then how could he, when she had only just discovered it for herself?

During the rest of the long drive back to the Peak, Venetia sat and thought about the man beside her. Whenever she had considered marriage she had never been able to envisage the person who would make her eager for it, beyond the fact that he would have to be well-educated and able to share her cultural interests. Apart from that, he had remained a nebulous figure. Certainly she had never thought he would be a married man, nor one who was still so in love with his wife that he only saw his idealised image of her, and not the person she really was. But there was another emotion to be added to his love: his guilt at causing the death of his and Margot's child. How deep that guilt must be if it allowed him to accept the invidiousness of his position.

Venetia sighed. Neil's kisses had been born of physical desire only: caused by his need of a woman rather than by a desire for a particular one. Any girl would have sufficed so long as he knew he could rely on her discretion. But he was wrong in one important aspect as far as she herself was concerned: she wanted more than a love based on sexual need, and since he could not offer more than this, she must put him out of her mind. And equally important, she must make sure he did not guess how she felt about him.

'You haven't answered me, Venetia.' His voice broke the silence. 'You do believe it won't happen again?'

'You kissing me?' She managed a light laugh. 'Of course I believe it.'

'And you'll stay for as long as I—as long as I need you?'

'I'll stay for as long as I can.' She peered through the window. 'We're at the house. I hadn't realised we'd arrived.'

He nodded without replying, and almost before the car stopped he opened the door and jumped out, as if he could no longer bear their proximity.

Slowly she followed him into the house, but by the time she entered the hall he was nowhere to be seen. She went to her room and sat on the bed, slipping off her shoes and flexing her toes on the carpet. Her movements were automatic, her thoughts still so preoccupied with Neil and the discovery of her love for him, that the knock on her door and the entering of Margot's maid, a young Chinese girl, took her by surprise.

'Mees Adams telephone to say she no be back for dinner,' the girl intoned. 'You please tell Mister?'

'Why don't you do it yourself?'

'Mees Adams ask me ask you do it.'

Venetia hid her dislike of the task ahead. After all, there was no point in disclosing her feelings to the maid, and with a nod of dismissal she went downstairs again in search of Neil. The thought of having to dine alone with him was intolerable, though less so than having dinner in her room and causing him to wonder why she did not wish to face him.

Even as she entered the library and spoke to Neil, a solution presented itself in the form of a telephone call from

Simon. Neil picked up the receiver, though he at once held it out in her direction.

'I've been trying to get you all day,' Simon complained. 'Where have you been?'

She gave a non-committal answer and he was quick to realise she was being overheard. 'Are you free for dinner tonight?'

'Yes, I am.'

'Then I'll collect you in half an hour.'

'Make it an hour. That will give me time to have a bath.'

Replacing the telephone, Venetia saw Neil watching her. He was leaning against the mantelpiece, one hand restlessly drumming the top of it. 'So I'm the one to be left by myself tonight,' he said lightly.

Recollecting the imperturbable way he had received the news that Margot was dining with Boris, she felt a surge of anger against him. 'You're dining alone from choice, Neil.'

'What other choice do I have?'

'You could act like a man!'

He tensed angrily. 'I told you once before not to judge me.'

'How can you be so calm about Margot?' she burst out. 'At least put up a fight!'

'It would be a waste of time.'

'Isn't there *something* you can do?'

'I've already told you that all I can do is to be here when she needs me.'

'And if she doesn't need you again?'

'She will.' His lips were tight and narrow. 'She always does. Boris is not the first, you know. Nor will he be the last.'

'And you just——' Venetia fought for words—'you just act dumb and accept it.'

'Yes.'

With an exclamation she swung out of the room. If Neil was prepared to put up with Margot's unfaithfulness and drunkenness then he deserved her. To be so guilty because of a car accident and a miscarriage was a neurotic refusal to face facts.

In her bedroom she expended some of her anger in scrubbing herself furiously under the shower, as if the rough brush could sweep away the memory of this afternoon. Then she searched out and put on her prettiest dress and applied more make-up than usual to hide her pallor and haunted eyes. She was pinning a diamond-studded comb into her dark hair when she heard Simon's car crunch to a stop in the drive, and picking up a mohair stole she ran down to intercept him before he could ring the doorbell.

But she was too late, for when she reached the hall he was already talking to Neil. What a contrast the two men made—one of medium height, though tall for a Chinese, with straight black hair, almond eyes and a sallow skin— and the other so tall and thin and blond, his movements spare, his expression indifferently polite in contrast with Simon's wide grin.

'You look beautiful, Venetia,' he said, hurrying over to greet her. 'But then you don't need to make any effort.'

'You should see my make-up drawer,' she smiled.

'Only lipstick,' he protested, 'the rest is you.' Tucking her arm through his, he drew her to the door, pausing while she said goodnight to Neil, who returned it calmly and was already halfway back to the library before she was out of the house.

As they sped down towards sea level, her heart was still with Neil, and it required a conscious effort to forget him and concentrate on the man beside her.

'You're so elusive these days,' he was complaining. 'Each time I telephone, you make an excuse not to see me. I was surprised you agreed to come out with me tonight.'

'I'm here to look after Margot,' she said, and amended hastily: 'It's my duty to be around when she wants me.'

'You're not her slave. I assume you *do* have some time off?'

'Of course I do. Neil said——'

'Neil, is it?' Simon's voice was sharp. 'I didn't know you were on Christian name terms.'

'Margot suggested it,' she said evenly.

'And where's the lovely lady tonight?'

Uncertain whether he knew Margot was out of the house, she decided it was unwise to lie. 'She's out—dining with friends.'

'Without her husband?'

Venetia shrugged, implying that there was nothing unusual in this. But Simon was not easily fooled. 'With Boris, I bet. So that affair's still blowing hot.'

'You shouldn't jump to conclusions.'

'There's no jumping required. Margot and Boris laid the path out very neatly! Neither of them has made any attempt to hide their affair.'

'Do you mind if we change the subject?' Venetia knew her voice was strained, but she was beyond caring. If there was any further discussion about Neil and Margot and their way of behaving, she would scream. 'I came out with *you*,' she added quickly. 'Don't waste time talking about other people.'

'Well,' Simon said in delight, 'you *are* being charming!' He reached out and squeezed her hand, but she did not respond to it and he dropped it back in her lap and took the wheel again. 'I tried to get you earlier today,' he went on. 'I was hoping you would have dinner at my home and meet my father, but as I couldn't contact you until late I had to leave it.'

Venetia tried not to show her relief. The last thing in the world she wanted was to meet Simon's father. She instinctively knew he rarely took his girl-friends home, and for him to want to do so with her implied a seriousness which perturbed her. The knowledge that she loved Neil had awakened her to the problem that could arise if she allowed Simon to cherish false hopes about her, and she knew it would be less painful for him if she made it clear that they had no future together. But she would have to do so diplomatically. One could not turn down a proposal of marriage that had not yet been made.

'As it was too late to arrange dinner at home,' Simon continued, 'I'm taking you to Aberdeen instead. It's a fishing village on the south side of the island. The Tanka people live there. I think you'll find them interesting. None of them have ever lived anywhere except on boats—there's a rumour they get seasick if they walk on dry land!'

'You mean they live on the water the whole time?'

He nodded. 'Their sampans are so close together they just cross from one to the other. You can walk along them for a mile and never touch land. Even the school is on the water—and the doctor's consulting room too!'

'How incredible.' Her interest was real. 'Will we be dining in a sampan?'

He shook his head. 'They're too small. All the restaurants are on junks.'

'What an off-putting name!'

'Wait till you see them,' he advised. 'They are beautifully painted and decorated with fantastic patterns. They're made of sandalwood,' he added. 'That's how Hong Kong got its name.'

'You've lost me on that one.'

'Years ago the main harbour was full of sandalwood junks and the wood gave off such a fragrant smell that the Chinese called it Fragrant Harbour. In our language the words are Hueng Kong.'

'What a lovely story!' She half-sighed. 'I'd like to learn Chinese. It sounds a fascinating language.'

'It is. We don't have an alphabet in the European way. We have many thousands of symbols—called characters—and each one is capable of several different meanings.'

'I think I'd better stick to English and French,' she smiled. 'It would take me years just to learn pidgin Chinese!'

'Nonsense. You could manage very well if you learned about fifteen hundred symbols. Our newspapers don't use more than about three thousand.'

'Three thousand!' she gasped. 'And Europeans complain about a twenty-six-letter alphabet!'

'Don't be so faint-hearted. If you really put your mind to it, you could be speaking Chinese in a year. I can recommend an excellent teacher who——'

'I won't be staying here long enough to learn the language.' Seeing her opportunity to warn him of her plans, she took it. 'I'll be going back to England in a few months, Simon. Sooner, if Neil will let me.'

So eager was she to establish one particular point with Simon that she did not realise she had established another until he slowed the car and gave her a curious look.

'You make it sound as if Adams is preventing you from leaving. I thought you worked for his wife?'

'I do, but——' she moistened her lips—'but it was Neil who engaged me and—and as he paid my fare to come out here,' she went on brightly, 'I can't simply leave when I want to do so.'

Simon appeared satisfied with the explanation and once more began to talk of Hong Kong, keeping up a flow of amusing anecdotes—both of the past and the present—until they reached Aberdeen and boarded a large scarlet and green-painted junk. Lying on the dark waters and lit by coloured lanterns, with its prow rising high, it looked more like a huge, gaudy sea-serpent than a vessel which, in its day, had been used to bring home the fish and provide a livelihood whereby whole villages had existed; but now these junks were floating restaurants, serving the best seafood in the Far East.

Venetia left it to Simon to order the meal, and was delighted by the innumerable dishes of succulent fish and sauces that paraded before her in a seemingly never-ending stream. No sweet and sour fishballs here, with the ubiquitous fried noodles, but giant-sized prawns and shrimps and lobster claws rich with meat.

They had finished their meal and were sipping jasmine-scented tea when she noticed a group of English people sitting several tables away. She had seen them on her arrival, but only now did she become aware of them, and decided there was something familiar about the plump woman with grey hair who appeared to be the guest of honour. But not until the woman turned to look at her host did Venetia get a proper glimpse of her face.

'It's Lady Rogers!' she exclaimed.

'You know her?' Simon asked.

'Very well. Her brother, Sir William Blunden, is my godfather. Would you excuse me while I go over and say hello?'

Simon nodded and Venetia went across to speak to Lady Rogers, who greeted her with warm surprise.

'What a coincidence to see you here tonight, Venetia. You are on the top of my list of people I'm going to call in the morning. I only arrived a couple of hours ago.' She introduced Venetia to the other people at the table. They were all from the large cruise ship anchored in Victoria Harbour, and were spending the next three days in Hong Kong.

'I wish Beeby had written and told me you were coming,' Venetia said, giving the older woman another hug. 'But then he hasn't written to me at all since I've been here.'

'Because he knows you're cross with him,' his sister said. 'He told me very particularly to look you up and give you his love.' Lady Rogers glanced over Venetia's shoulder. 'Why not bring your friend over and join us for coffee?'

Venetia was delighted at the idea, and so was Simon, who was immediately at ease with everyone and found himself plied with questions as to where one could obtain the best antiques and jewellery. He was in his element, proffering advice and caution, and seeing he was happily occupied, Venetia was able to talk quietly to Dorothy Rogers.

'You're looking rather strained,' the older woman commented. 'Still, I'm not surprised. I told William he had no business sending you out here without warning you about Margot.'

'You know about——?'

'Half London knows—and the whole of Somerset! It

really was very naughty of William not to tell you. But then he was quite deliberate about it. He can be a most unscrupulous man, you know.'

Venetia's nod was heartfelt, and gave away more than she had intended.

'Don't become involved in Margot's and Neil's problems,' Lady Rogers advised. 'No one can do anything for them.'

'But they're so unhappy together.'

'They'd be unhappier apart—at least Margot would. That's why Neil won't leave her.'

'He doesn't stay with Margot because *she* wants him to,' Venetia corrected, 'but because he loves her and blames himself for the accident.'

'It isn't *his* guilt that ties Neil to Margot—it's hers! And I doubt if he loves her either. I know he doted on her when they got married, but she quickly put paid to that. No one can love Margot for long: she's too unstable. Neil would have seen it himself if he hadn't been so naïve. It's amazing how stupid a clever man can be when it comes to a pretty woman.'

Venetia hesitated and then allowed her curiosity full rein. 'What do you mean about Margot being guilty and not Neil?'

'I thought you said he told you about the accident?'

'Margot told me.'

'I see.' Lady Rogers sighed. 'I should have realised Neil wouldn't say anything. And as my dear brother didn't see fit to do so . . .' The brown eyes flickered across the table, making sure everyone was engaged in conversation, before settling back on Venetia. 'As you're living with them—and looking none too happy because of it—I think you should know the whole story.'

Venetia waited tensely, uncertain how it could differ from the one she already knew.

'The accident was Margot's fault entirely,' Lady Rogers went on. 'Neil had nothing to do with it.'

'Nothing to . . .' Venetia frowned. 'Then why did he take the blame?'

'Because of everything that had happened before. Margot's a twin, you know, and she was devoted to her brother. Everyone was. He had all Margot's charm and none of her moods. He was killed in a skiing accident and his body was flown home from Switzerland. Margot was pregnant at the time and in bed with influenza. Her doctor refused to let her go to the funeral, but she absolutely insisted and forced Neil to drive her there. It was a terrible February day and they had to go cross-country for several miles. She became angry with Neil for driving too slowly and she grabbed the wheel. He wouldn't let her take it and she went into a rage and got hysterical. She's famous for her rages—they call it the Destry Inheritance. Anyway, she started hitting Neil and tried to climb into the driving seat. The car went out of control and they crashed.'

For a long moment Venetia was silent, absorbing all she had just learned. Margot's recounting of the accident did not tally with Lady Rogers'. Yet she knew instinctively that Margot had not been lying. There had been no sly look to mar the beauty of her face as she had told her story, only a deep, vindictive and utterly real hatred for Neil.

'Margot said it was Neil's fault,' she murmured, 'and I'm sure she was speaking the truth.'

'The truth as she knows it,' Lady Rogers said. 'Except that it doesn't happen to be the truth! She lost her memory after the accident and she doesn't remember a thing about it. Neil refused to tell her what happened and he still won't do so.'

It was several seconds before Venetia could absorb what she had just learned. 'But why?' she muttered. 'I can see why Neil kept quiet immediately after the accident . . . but not afterwards. It doesn't make sense.'

'Not to you and me perhaps, because we're hard-headed creatures—women are, you know. We're much more logical than men, despite what they say to the contrary. When it comes to sentiment, you can't beat a man!'

'You mean Neil is being sentimental?'

'*He* thinks he's being logical. When William spoke to him about telling Margot the truth, he said she'd crack up completely if she knew *she'd* caused it. For three months after the accident she was terribly ill. She was in a private nursing home and Neil danced attendance on her. But a fortnight after she returned home the Prime Minister sent him to India. He was gone two months—much longer than he had planned—and Margot refused to join him. When he came back he discovered she had started to drink heavily, and of course that made him even more afraid to tell her the truth.'

'So being Neil he decided to wait until she was better.'

Lady Rogers blinked at the anger in Venetia's voice. 'That's exactly it. Except that Margot didn't get better; in fact her drinking and her wild behaviour almost ruined his career.'

'She *wants* to ruin it,' Venetia said bluntly. 'She told me so. It's because she blames Neil for her losing the baby.'

Lady Rogers shook her head worriedly. 'I didn't know she still felt so badly. I had hoped—we'd *all* hoped—that she would eventually regard the accident as—well, fate if you like. Something that could have happened at any time.'

'She hates Neil as much now as she did when she woke up in the hospital,' Venetia said firmly, 'and if he won't tell her the truth, she'll go on hating him.'

'He'll never tell her. William begged him to do so before he came to Hong Kong, but he refused.' Lady Rogers frowned. 'I wish *you* could make him see sense.'

'He wouldn't listen to me,' Venetia said hastily. 'He's blind where Margot's concerned. He *does* love her—despite what you say. He wouldn't be willing to sacrifice his career if he didn't.'

'It's because he *doesn't* love her that he's sacrificing himself! Margot didn't want a child and only agreed to have one because she knew it would keep Neil tied to her. But she resented every minute of the pregnancy—that's why she insisted on dashing across the countryside to attend poor

Tommy's funeral. After all, she couldn't bring her brother back, and she should have given some thought to the baby she was carrying. Neil's positive she insisted on getting up in order to spite him; to show him that though she was pregnant it wasn't going to make any difference to her life.'

'It sounds highly dramatic and far-fetched,' Venetia said warily.

'Margot *is*!'

In view of the girl's reckless relationship with Boris, the remark could not be gainsaid. But there was no point bringing the Russian into the conversation, and deciding to end it before she gave away her own feelings, Venetia stood up. At once Simon came to stand beside her.

'Will you come and see me again while I'm here?' Lady Rogers asked. 'We're all going sightseeing tomorrow, but we're having dinner at the Peninsula. Come and join us.'

'Neil's giving a dinner party tomorrow,' Venetia said, 'and I think he'll want me to remain with Margot.'

'Then perhaps we can meet the day after. Call me, my dear.'

Promising to do so, Venetia left with Simon, and the moment they were alone together in his car he commented on her lengthy conversation with Lady Rogers.

'You looked completely spellbound. Was it good news or bad?'

'Only gossip from home,' she lied. 'And it's made me terribly homesick. I guess I'll never be happy living away from England.'

'I can't believe that.' He caught her hand. 'I was hoping you would consider remaining in Hong Kong. You know how I feel about you.'

'Please, Simon.' She drew her hand away. 'Don't say any more. It won't do any good.'

'Is it because I'm Chinese?'

'Because you're——' Aghast, she stared at him. 'Oh *no*, certainly not!'

'Then are you in love with someone else?'

'No.' She made her voice firm, knowing he would continue to pry unless she could convince him. Her tone must have done the trick, for he accepted her denial and chatted lightly about nothing in particular, until they drew up outside the Adams' house.

'When can I see you again?' he asked, walking with her to the steps.

'I'll telephone you.'

'Is that a promise or a brush-off?'

'A promise, Simon.'

'Good.' He kissed her gently on the cheek and waited while she unlocked the front door and then closed it behind her.

Moving quietly across the hall, she heard the sound of raised voices.

'You can't stop me going away with Boris,' Margot was saying. 'I won't let you ruin the rest of my life.'

'I'm trying to *stop* you from ruining it!' Neil's voice was sharper than Venetia had ever heard it, and hurriedly she tiptoed towards the stairs.

'*You* ruined my life,' Margot screamed. 'And now you're trying to stop me being happy with another man.'

'You'll never be happy with Kanin.'

'I'll never be happy with you! I'm leaving you, Neil. I'll be hostess at your stupid party, but that's the last thing I'm going to do for you. I'm leaving the day after tomorrow.' There was the sound of a chair scraping on the floor, a door was flung wide and Margot came running into the hall. 'Venetia!' she cried. 'Thank heavens you're back!'

Flinging herself against Venetia, she burst into tears, and over the downbent red head Venetia looked up and saw Neil watching from the doorway. His face seemed as if carved from marble, and without a word he turned back into the room and closed the door behind him.

Gently Venetia guided Margot up the stairs to her room. Her uncontrollable sobbing had ceased, though she did not speak until she was in bed and lying back against the pillows, her luminous eyes still brilliant with tears, her thin body softened by diaphanous chiffon. She was even thinner than Venetia had realised, as though she was being burned up by the intensity of her emotions. Looking at her it was easy to see why Neil could not bear to tell her the truth. The thin clutching hands, the bright eyes—so defiant one minute, so hauntingly childlike the next—all bespoke a nervous system teetering on the edge of insanity.

Despite the fact that Margot had not wanted to have a child, how would she react to the knowledge that she herself had wrenched the wheel which had caused the accident? No, Venetia decided soberly, if she were in Neil's place she would not be able to tell Margot the truth either. But nor could she have stood by and condoned her love affairs. Lady Rogers must be wrong in her assessment of Neil's feelings. He had to love Margot. If he didn't, surely he would gladly let her go to Boris?

'I suppose you know about the dinner party,' Margot said petulantly. 'Thank heavens it will be the last time I'll have to play hostess for him.'

Venetia smoothed the sheets but remained silent, and the glittering eyes watched her. 'You think I'm horrible to Neil, don't you?'

'I try not to think of it at all.'

'Because you don't like condemning him! You're loyal, Venetia, I'll say that for you. A loyal, cold fish.' The glitter was more pronounced and so was the petulance. 'You and Neil are very much alike. Neither of you can understand my kind of love. That you can want someone so desperately that you'll do anything—*anything*—in order to be with them.'

'I am well aware of the power of love,' Venetia replied. 'But I hope I would have enough sense not to let it destroy me.'

'Do *you* think Boris is wrong for me too?'

'I don't like Mr Kanin, as you know. But even apart from personal prejudice, I do think he's the wrong man for you.'

'Because he isn't a true-blue British aristocrat!'

'Because he isn't kind.'

'Kindness!' Margot cried. 'Neil's kind and I hate him.'

'Then you don't deserve him.' Venetia straightened and gave the sheet a sharp tug. 'Goodnight, Margot.' She was at the door when the lilting voice called her back.

'You're always so quick to defend Neil. Perhaps you're in love with him yourself?'

Venetia was glad her hand was on the doorknob because it helped her to keep steady. 'I'd love any man who could put up with you,' she said calmly, and closed the door behind her.

CHAPTER ELEVEN

YET another sleepless night found Venetia greeting the day with heavy eyes, and she listlessly descended the stairs to find the house awash with servants. Several were in the dining room busy with silver and linen, and she saw that the long table had been extended even further. A quick count of the place settings told her there would be some twenty guests. Margot would be in her element playing hostess to such a gathering, unless her dislike of Neil made her decide to ruin the evening for him.

Pushing the disquieting thought aside, she went into the drawing room. Numerous bowls of flowers had been placed around the room, and automatically she altered the position of some of the bowls, softening the hard lines of the mantelpiece with a cluster of irises and daffodils. As she moved back to look at it, her eyes saw Neil's reflection in the mirror, and she jumped so violently that it was impossible to hide the movement.

'I'm sorry if I startled you,' he apologised. 'I came in to make sure everything was in order.'

'There's no need for you to worry if the details are all right,' she said quietly. 'I'll make sure they are.'

'The dinner menu has already been arranged.'

There was no need for him to tell her he had done it himself. Anger against Margot raced up in her, and she knew it was going to be impossible for her to see this assignment through. No matter how much she denied her love for Neil, no matter how frequently she reminded herself that he had eyes for no one except his wife, she would not be able to overcome her bitterness that he could remain in love with someone who could throw it back in his face in the most hurtful way possible.

'A penny for your thoughts, Venetia,' he said suddenly.

'They're not worth that much.'

'Don't undervalue yourself.' His brows drew together. 'You're the least conceited woman I have ever met.'

Compared with Margot anyone would be, she thought, but knew better than to say so.

'You get things done with the minimum of fuss,' he went on. 'It's only when I start to think about it that I realise what a difference you've made to the house.'

'I've done nothing,' she said in surprise.

'You do the flowers each day. You've persuaded the cook to vary the menu—which must have required masterly diplomacy. You've even mover the furniture around in the drawing room and study.'

'I thought you hadn't noticed.'

'I notice everything you do.' His voice was unexpectedly husky. 'I notice the way you walk—so quick and graceful. The way you talk. The way——'

'Don't flirt with me!' she cried. 'You've no right to do so.'

He was silent for so long that she was forced to turn and look at him. There was a faint shine of sweat on his forehead and his eyes were so pale that they looked like chips of ice.

'Am I so different from Simon Hoy?' he asked at last. 'I've noticed you've no objection to flirting with *him*.'

'He isn't married! That makes all the difference. I don't want to be your girl-friend, Neil. If you want someone to go to bed with, you must look somewhere else!'

'Venetia, don't say that!'

'Why not? It's true, isn't it?'

He took a step towards her, but she evaded his grasp and ran wildly from the room, quite different from the gentle creature he had described a moment ago.

Anxious to escape him, she ran to Margot's room, clutching the post and a parcel of books. Margot was talking on the telephone to Boris, telling him of the dinner party and the dress she was going to wear. It was idle chat which Venetia could not imagine he would be interested in, yet he appeared to be saying the right things, for the lilting voice went on endlessly, saying far more than she should have done about the people who were coming, and how important the dinner was to Neil.

'I'll tell you more about it this afternoon, darling,' she said, concluding the conversation. 'As it's the last time I'll be Neil's hostess, I intend to make it an unforgettable occasion.' She was smiling slightly as she put down the telephone, though the smile faded as she saw Venetia's face. 'Still judging me?' she snapped.

'I'm not judging you.'

'But you disapprove of what I'm doing, don't you?'

'Is it necessary to have this discussion again?' Venetia perched on the edge of a chair. 'If you're leaving Hong Kong you won't be needing me any more.'

'I want you to stay with me till I go.'

'I thought you were leaving tomorrow?'

'It may not be until the end of the week—or next week, even. Boris is waiting to hear from someone.'

Unable to stop herself, Venetia went over to the bed. Though she believed it was in Margot and Neil's best interests for them to part if they could not live amicably together, she agreed with Neil that Boris was the wrong man to take his place. 'Are you sure you're doing the right thing, Margot?' she asked. 'How well do you know Boris?'

'Well enough to know I love him.'

'Does he love you?'

'What a stupid question! He's asked me to go away with him—to marry me when I'm free. Doesn't that sound like love even to your prissy little mind?'

Angrily Margot pushed her hair away from her face. It threw the beautiful bone structure into relief and highlighted the translucent quality of her skin. More than ever Venetia sensed that the woman was living on her nerves, and that only the excitement she engendered around herself gave her the energy to keep going. Margot enjoyed her flirtation with Boris as much as she enjoyed taunting Neil, but somehow neither emotion seemed genuine. Perhaps a woman who drank heavily was unable to be genuine about anything?

'You've a tiring evening ahead.' Venetia tried to keep any criticism from her voice. 'I thought it might be a good idea for us to spend the day around the house. Some books have arrived from England and this afternoon——'

'This afternoon I'm seeing Boris, so shut up and get out!'

Venetia went to obey the command, but a thin hand came out and clutched her arm.

'What a bitch I am!' Margot cried. 'Don't leave me, Venetia. You're the only person who keeps me sane.'

Venetia clenched her hands at her sides, glad that her face was turned away from Margot's. 'You won't be needing me when you leave here,' she said stiffly, 'but until you—until you go, I'll stay.'

Only when she was in the corridor did Venetia release her own anger. What a fool she was to have agreed to remain here until Margot went away with Boris. Yet there was something pathetic about Margot that made it impossible to dislike her. How easy it was to see why Neil could not bring himself to leave her either. But what would happen to him when Margot left of her own accord? Would he go on pining for her, or would he set her free and try to make another life for himself? But what sort of life could he offer a woman when his heart was still with another one?

I couldn't accept him on those terms, Venetia said to herself. Better not to have him at all than to share him with a ghost that can never be laid.

Downstairs again, she saw that the table had been set and silver and glass gleamed amidst bowls of red roses: a compliment to the guests, which she was sure stemmed from Neil. For all the interest Margot had taken in the preparations for the dinner she might as well not be here. Yet her presence tonight seemed terribly important to Neil, and Venetia wondered why.

Luncheon was a hurried affair which she and Margot

took in the drawing room on a trolley, and as soon as it was over Margot announced that she was going to see Boris.

'What time will you be back?' Venetia asked.

'Don't worry, darling. I've told you I'm going to make this a memorable swansong for my devoted husband.' She glided from the room as lightly as a young girl going to her first party, leaving Venetia to wonder again how Neil could have fallen in love with someone so different from himself. Yet it was said that opposites attract, and perhaps it was Margot's very differences which had drawn him to her.

Unwilling to sit and think about him, she tried to find herself some work to do. But her notebook was empty and all her letters done. To call herself a social secretary was a joke, for apart from the one charity luncheon which Margot had arranged, she had done nothing else since Venetia's arrival in Hong Kong. To dispel her restlessness she decided to go for a walk. The view at least would take her mind off her thoughts, making her aware of the great big world that existed outside this unhappy household.

Venetia remained out longer than she had intended, and it was well after five when she returned home. Margot's car and chauffeur were not in the drive and she hurried upstairs to the bedroom. This was empty too, and she ran down to the kitchen in search of Yim. He had not seen Margot and, unable to prevent herself, she dialled Boris's flat. The telephone was picked up almost at once, as though he had been expecting a call, though his voice was lazily casual as he recognised Venetia's.

'Is Margot with you?' she said without preamble. 'She has people arriving at seven and she must get dressed.'

'At the moment she can't even get to her feet.'

'What do you mean?'

'What do you think I mean?' His voice was still slow, giving an instant picture of him swaying slightly on the balls of his feet, black eyes sardonic, head thrown back in contempt.

'You haven't allowed her to—you didn't give her anything to drink, did you, Boris?'

'Come and see for yourself,' he said, and quietly put down the receiver.

Not stopping to think, Venetia ran into the little room beside the kitchen where Yim did his ironing. He was lovingly pressing a navy suit but put the iron down at the sight of her face. 'I must go to Mr Kanin's apartment at once,' she explained. 'There isn't time to call a taxi. Do any of the servants have a car?'

He put up a reassuring hand and disappeared into the kitchen, coming back almost at once with a young boy. 'San has a car. He is parked at back of house. I tell him to bring to front.'

'There's no time. Come on!' she called over her shoulder, and ran through the kitchen to the back door.

An old car was parked near the shrubbery, and urging the young man to drive as quickly as he could, Venetia climbed in and gave him Boris's address. He did not ask for directions but immediately headed for the mid-level, and after going for a couple of miles swung off the main road to stop outside a new block of apartment houses.

'Wait for me,' she ordered, and ignoring the lift, raced up the three flights.

Hardly had she put her finger on the bell when Boris opened the door. In black slacks and white silk shirt, which heightened the breadth of his shoulders, he exuded a virile magnetism. 'You got here even quicker than I thought you would.'

He was smiling, and remained smiling as she pushed past him and went into the sitting room. It did not need the smell of whisky to tell her what had happened, nor the sight of the comatose figure and the flowing red hair that fell back from the slack face.

Fury such as she had never felt before engulfed Venetia, and she swung round and hit Boris across the chest. 'You rotten swine! How could you do such a thing to her?'

With a large hand he caught Venetia's two, removing them from him as though they were flies. 'She did it to herself,' he said pleasantly. 'Margot makes her own destruction.'

'You encouraged her. *Someone* has to give her the first drink. She never takes it on her own.'

His laugh was scornful. 'Margot's been drunk by herself more times than I've seen years. She's a dipsomaniac, Venetia. She'll drink anything when the mood takes her.'

'But she wasn't in that sort of mood today. She was looking forward to tonight.'

'She had no intention of being there. I assure you of that.'

The words took a moment to register, but when they did, Venetia suddenly realised what sense they made. This was what Margot had meant when she had said she was going to make her last dinner party for Neil a memorable occasion. This was the final blow she had planned for his ego. What bigger fool could one make of a man than to make a fool of him in his own home?

'Carry her to the car,' she ordered. 'I'm taking her home.'

'You'll never get her into a fit state for tonight. Neil's Chinese guests will have to manage without a hostess.' Boris's teeth flashed in a wolfish grin. 'It will be interesting to see what explanation he makes to Lai-Kin.'

'Lai-Kin?' she queried.

'The leader of the delegation. You haven't been doing your homework, I see. I'm afraid he's going to take Margot's absence as an insult.'

'I don't see why he should. Neil will tell him she's ill.'

'Lai-Kin won't accept that explanation. He's always looking for slights—especially from European women. Margot's absence tonight will do her husband no good.'

'What do you mean?'

'Ask our fair diplomat.' Boris sat down in an armchair.

Venetia stared from him to Margot, supine on the settee, then she bent over and tugged at the thin shoulders. Slight though she was, the woman was too heavy for her to lift, and she straightened, flushed and panting. 'If you won't help me,' she glared at Boris, 'I'll get San.' She turned to the front door, but found her way barred.

'Who's San?' Boris asked.

'The servant who brought me here. Now get out of my way while I fetch him.'

Admiration glinted in the small brown eyes. 'Why are you doing all this? For love of country or love of man?'

'I'm more interested in why *you've* done it. Is it hatred of Margot or hatred of Neil?'

'Neither.'

Not pausing to analyse his reply, she went to push past him, but he caught her arm and pulled her back. 'I'll bring her out,' he said tersely, and as easily as though Margot were a feather pillow, he picked her up, carried her down to the waiting car and placed her in the back.

Without looking at him, Venetia got in beside the driver and ordered the young Chinese to return to the house as fast as he could.

The blue hour of dusk lay gently around them as San and Yim carried Margot up to her room. She was still unconscious and breathing heavily. It looked as though Boris might well be right and she would be impossible to awaken, yet Venetia was determined not to give in and, thankful she had made a note of Margot's doctor, she telephoned him.

'Have you tried to rouse her?' he asked.

'I've done everything I can think of, but she's dead to the world.'

'Then it doesn't look promising. If you could get her to open her eyes you might be able to walk her around.'

'She's completely unconscious.'

'Then you'll have to let her sleep it off.'

'What about an injection?' Venetia pleaded. 'There must be something you can do.'

'Injections are dangerous and her heart isn't strong enough.'

'Her heart? I didn't know.'

'Mr Adams does,' the doctor said quietly. 'I suggest you leave her be.'

Venetia walked back to the bed and stared at the sleeping figure. Chaotic thoughts tumbled about in her brain, but she could not make sense of them, and she was still standing there, uneasy and confused, when she felt Neil come to stand beside her.

She lifted her head and looked at him. 'I'm sorry. I tried to stop her going to Boris, but she wouldn't listen to me.'

'She never listens to anyone.' His mouth narrowed into a bitter line. 'I should have realised this was what she was going to do. She never had any intention of acting as my hostess tonight.'

'If you suspected that, why didn't you stay with her today?'

'I had documents to prepare for this evening. It was impossible for me to remain at home.'

'You could have taken her with you.'

'Could you have seen her coming?' he asked furiously. 'No one tells Margot what to do—least of all me!'

'It's a pity you arranged to hold the dinner party here in the first place.'

'Do you think I *wanted* to? Lai-Kin asked to come here. I told you that.'

'And now he'll see your wife's absence as an insult.'

'You know?' Neil said sharply.

'Boris said something about it.'

'Kanin?' Neil looked astounded. 'So *he's* at the bottom of all this.'

'All what?' Venetia was puzzled and showed it.

'Margot's getting drunk,' he explained. 'Kanin must have put the idea into her head.'

'He said he couldn't stop her.'

'I bet he didn't even try. He *wanted* her to get drunk.'

She nodded, remembering some of the things Boris had said. 'Why will Lai-Kin regard Margot's absence as an insult? If you explain that she's ill ...'

'I spoke to him this morning and said that Margot was particularly looking forward to meeting him tonight.' Neil's expression was bleak. 'He'll never believe her indisposition is genuine.'

'Why not?'

'Because he's always on the look-out for an insult from a white woman.'

Venetia blinked. 'You're joking?'

'It's hardly a joking matter.'

'But why should he expect a white woman to insult him?'

Neil moved back so violently that he knocked against a chair. It slithered across the carpet and came to rest with a sharp bang against the wardrobe. But nothing disturbed the unconscious figure on the bed and he flung it a look of anguish before he began to pace the room. 'Lai-Kin's a peasant. A highly-educated man, but a peasant by birth and background. It's an uneasy combination and makes him suspicious of pure intellectuals and the aristocracy—what he refers to as the governing classes.' Neil drew a deep breath. 'He came to England to study and fell in love with the daughter of a baronet. They planned to marry, but at the last moment she ran away. She didn't have the courage to face him, but left him a letter instead. He carries it around with him still and shows it to his closest friends. They all treat the whole thing as a joke, but of course it isn't. Lai-Kin has never forgiven her for saying she was afraid to marry him because she didn't want to have yellow children!'

Venetia's gasp of horror was audible and Neil grimaced as he heard it.

'You can see now why he expects white women to insult him.'

'Yes,' she murmured, 'I'm afraid I can. It seems to me you'll have to tell him the truth.'

'That my wife's a drunk and hates me?'

'Isn't it better to lose *your* face than to let Lai-Kin believe he's lost his? Which he *will* feel if he thinks Margot has deliberately refused to meet him.'

Neil rubbed his fingers across his forehead. 'I suppose you're right. It's the lesser of two evils, though either way it's going to put a blight on this evening. Not that I care for my own loss of face,' he added, 'but the talks are going so well ... There's only one major difference between us and I was hoping we could settle it tonight.'

There was a knock at the door and Margot's maid came in, her arms full of oyster satin. 'Mees Adams' dress,' she said sibilantly.

'I'll take it.' Venetia quickly did so, pushing the girl back into the hall again before she caught sight of Neil's ravaged face. Still clasping the satin, she came back into the centre of the room. 'You'd better change, Neil. There's no point in your being late.' He did not answer and she went to the wardrobe to take out a hanger. Careful not to let the hem of the dress touch the carpet, she held it against her and was reaching into the wardrobe when Neil's sudden shout made her jump.

'*You* can do it!' he cried. 'You're the same height and almost the same figure. *You* can be Margot tonight!'

She stared at him blankly and he came over and took the dress from her nerveless fingers, holding it up against her and then dragging her over to the dressing table. 'Put it on and pretend you're Margot,' he ordered. 'None of the Chinese delegation has seen her and they'll never know the truth.'

'But the servants—your own delegation?'

'There's only my assistant and myself. The rest are Lai-Kin's party. You've got to do it, Venetia. It's the best possible solution.'

'I can't.' She moistened lips that were suddenly dry. 'How can you ask me to pretend to be your wife?'

'Is it so impossible for you to imagine it for just a few hours?' He spoke so bitterly that she turned away from the sight of his face. If only he knew what he was asking of her. If only he knew how much she wished that it were not a pretence.

'Very well,' she said shakily. 'I'll do it.'

CHAPTER TWELVE

DISBELIEVINGLY Venetia stared at her reflection in the mirror. If anyone ever again told her that fine feathers did not make a fine bird, she would tell them to have their head examined!

The dress had looked magnificent on Margot, but without conceit she knew it looked even better on herself. Though she had been worried that Margot's slenderness might have made the dress too tight, she had been amazed to find it fitted her almost like a second skin. All that had been required was to take out the padding in the bust and so give room for her own breasts, which needed no falseness to project their swelling curves. The oyster-coloured satin lent pink warmth to her pale skin and set off the dramatic blackness of her hair, which gleamed as brilliantly as the lustre of the full skirts that swirled around her feet. She had not known how graceful was the column of her throat, nor how pure the line of her shoulders until she saw them framed by the simple folds of the wide collar, which met beneath her breasts and formed itself into a bow.

The stark simplicity of the style called for equal simplicity of make-up, and she had used only lipstick and mascara. It made her lashes look absurdly long and they stuck out so thick and straight that she wondered if they did not make her look childish. Yet if they did, it was a childishness all the more provocative because of the elegance to which it was allied; an elegance echoed by her thick, straight hair, which she let fall loosely to her shoulders. No doubting her Irish grandmother tonight, she thought as she went nervously down the stairs: a chatelaine without a castle; a wife without a husband.

Only as she reached the bottom step and raised her eyes did she become aware of Neil watching her, and a pulse started in her throat as though a bird was there fighting to be free.

For a moment he looked at her without speaking, but his expression made words unnecessary, and she knew he found her beautiful. It brought to mind a picture of the lonely nights he must spend. No wonder he was looking at her with such longing. Furious with him, she wanted to hurt him and said the first thing that came into her mind. 'Your wife in name only, Neil. Remember that.'

'You're determined to make sure I don't forget it.'

'Men who play around should never play around the home!'

Colour flamed his cheeks and he took a step forward. Then his control reasserted itself and he moved away again.

'You need a necklace,' he said abruptly. 'Come into the library.'

She followed him, watching silently as from a drawer in the desk he took out a black leather case. A row of glowing rubies and diamonds lay between his fingers and he held them out to her. She took them and went to put them on, but the collar of her dress got in the way and, avoiding looking at him, she handed them back and asked him to fasten them on for her. He came behind her and she felt his fingers on the nape of her neck as he closed the clasp. He did not move away from her at once, but remained close, his breath fanning her cheek.

'You're a very beautiful woman, Venetia. I always knew you were, but tonight you—you take my breath away.'

She was saved from replying by the scrunch of cars on the driveway, and he immediately turned to the door. With fast-beating heart she went to stand beside him.

'Don't forget your name is Margot,' he warned, as Yim crossed the hall in front of them.

Too nervous to do more than nod, she watched as the Chinese delegates came quietly in. They were not at all as she had imagined they would be. Though they all wore identical costumes of narrow trousers and plain, well-fitting tunics, they had nothing of the spartan simplicity of manner she had expected, and were friendly and talkative, all of them speaking English, and most of them doing so very fluently.

Drinks were served in the drawing room and Venetia moved from group to group, managing to keep the conversation on a friendly but impersonal level, and avoiding any topic which could lead to her being asked any questions she might have found difficult to answer.

Lai-Kin spoke only a few words of greeting to her, but at dinner she was aware of his dark eyes frequently staring at her and then sliding away, almost as if he were waiting for her to say something to which he could take exception. The thought of this reminded her of the deception she and Neil were playing on him, and she trembled so acutely that she had to set her fork down on her plate.

'You do not like Chinese food?' Lai-Kin asked, swift as a scorpion.

For a brief instant she hesitated. The man was far too perceptive for her to lie to him, and though she was carrying out a magnificent lie by pretending to be Margot, she could only maintain the charade if she did not have to lie about anything else. She was Margot in name, but she was going to be Venetia in character.

'I love Chinese food,' she said shakily.

'Then why are you not eating?'

'Nerves, I suppose. I often lose my appetite when I'm frightened.'

'Ah.' The sound was disbelieving, as were his sloe eyes, which she forced herself to look into. 'You are not suggesting you are frightened by this dinner party?'

'I'm petrified,' she admitted.

'But you are a well-known hostess. How can a few simple Chinese worry you?'

'Hardly simple, Your Excellency.' She forced a smile to her lips. 'It is easy to entertain people one knows, but——'

'Not easy to entertain people of a different class and colour?'

Venetia caught her breath. Lai-Kin had carried the ball

right into her court, and had hit it straight at her. Taking her courage in both hands, she hit it back to him. 'That's it exactly, Your Excellency. Even one's own countrymen can be difficult enough to understand, but people from another background take much more knowing. I'm sure you find *us* equally difficult?'

'I was educated in England,' he said coldly.

'Then you know at first hand how unfriendly we can be!'

'Yes,' he said meaningly, 'I do. There is no one more suspicious and aloof than a British aristocrat.'

'Your own people can be aloof too,' she replied, remembering the last Chinese delegation that had come to London.

'You sound as if you are speaking from knowledge. Do you know many Chinese?'

'A few,' she replied. 'But I was actually quoting a friend of mine. She—she works for the Foreign Office in London and she had some problems with a group of your countrymen who came over on a visit.'

'You should come and see us in China, Mrs Adams. Never judge a race until you have been in their own country.'

'But the world is getting so small, Excellency, that people must learn to live in foreign environments yet retain their own identity.'

'Are you suggesting ghettoes for each race?'

Again she caught her breath, then said carefully: 'A person can create his own ghetto just by being self-conscious.'

'It is hard to be otherwise when one is made to feel different from other people.' His hand came out to rest on her arm. It was a small, almost boneless hand with yellowish skin. 'Yours is so white,' he said.

'Does it disgust you?'

He looked at her sharply. 'Why should it disgust me?'

'Because it's white and cold-looking and yours is golden and warm.'

'Are you teasing me, Mrs Adams?'

'Of course I am. You are yellow-skinned and I am white, but we are both members of the human race. Anyone who doesn't realise that is a fool.'

'There are millions of fools in the world.'

'I know that, and I am saddened by it. That's why I think it's important for everyone to talk out their differences—not run away from them.'

For what seemed an endless moment, Lai-Kin was silent. His face, impassive as all Oriental faces were, gave no indication of his thoughts. Then all at once he beamed—a wide and appraising smile that lit up his small features.

'You are as intelligent as you are beautiful, Mrs Adams. And you are very beautiful.'

'Thank you, Excellency. And I'm glad that all Western women do not look the same to you!'

At this he burst out laughing. 'It is good that we can smile at our differences.'

'It is the only way that differences can be overcome.'

'A toast,' said Lai-Kin, and getting to his feet he raised his glass in Neil's direction. 'To your wife, Neil Adams. A truly gracious and beautiful woman.'

All the men imediately rose and lifted their glasses and, scarlet-faced, Venetia stared at the bowl of flowers in front of her and wished she were a million miles away.

Neil did not have an opportunity to speak to her until they moved to the drawing room when dinner was over. 'I've never seen Lai-Kin laugh like that before,' he murmured. 'You went down like a bomb.'

'I only hope it won't explode in my face!'

'More likely in mine,' he said humorously. 'Still, things are going well, so far.'

'I'll leave you as soon as coffee has been served. I assume you want to start your talks?'

'Only if Lai-Kin gives the signal, not otherwise. But there won't be any need for you to leave. If we do talk, we'll go off to the study.'

Neil's hopes were justified, for hardly had he accepted a cup of coffee from the butler when Lai-Kin stood up, and immediately Neil led him out of the room.

Venetia remained, moving between the remaining men and doing her best to keep the conversation going. It was no easy task to make small talk with so many strangers, but she could see no way of escaping from it and manfully she struggled on.

Slowly an hour passed and then another, and she was wondering whether she would be able to carry on for much longer when Neil and Lai-Kin reappeared.

'I am sorry to have kept you up so late,' the Chinese said, coming to stand beside her. 'Next time we meet I hope you and your husband will be *my* guests.'

'I would be delighted,' she said formally.

'So will I. You are one of the few European women with whom I feel at ease—whom I feel I can trust.'

It was an unexpected admission, and knowing she was playing a charade made her extremely guilty. What would happen if he discovered she was not Neil's wife, but a secretary? He would certainly feel his trust had been misplaced and—even worse—taken advantage of. Some premonition—which afterwards she could never reason away—decided her to tell him the truth.

'I have a confession to make, Excellency. I am—I am not Margot Adams.'

'You are not ... This is a joke, perhaps?'

'It was no joke,' she said quickly. 'But Mrs Adams was ill and—and Neil felt you would be offended if she didn't appear at the dinner.'

'Why should I be offended because his wife was ill?'

Venetia moistened her lips. This was more difficult than she had anticipated. 'He was afraid you would not believe him. You had said you particularly wished to meet his wife and he—he thought you would feel slighted if he were unable to introduce her to you.'

'I would have found it strange,' he admitted. 'But one cannot legislate against illness.' As far as was possible in so inscrutable a man, Lai-Kin looked irritable. 'It would have been better to have told me the truth. I am not so insensitive that I would not have understood.'

'Your sensitivity was not in doubt, Excellency,' she said quietly. 'It was its depth that Neil found worrying.' Venetia regretted the impulse that had made her tell him the truth and she plunged on desperately. 'We know about your—of your unhappy experience when you were in England and—that was the reason. We felt you—we didn't want you to feel slighted. When a person has been hurt once ...'

'You are not suggesting I am *still* hurt by the past?'

'Yes,' she said quietly, 'I believe you are.'

'Then you take me for a fool!'

'I take you to be an over-sensitive man who was deeply hurt by an insensitive girl! A woman who really loved you would be proud to marry you. She'd never turn you down because you weren't a European. At dinner tonight you agreed with me when I said we are all human beings, no matter the colour of our skin. And human beings can make mistakes.' She plunged on, knowing it was too late for half measures. 'Your mistake—if you'll forgive me for saying so—is that you loved well, but not wisely!'

The silence between them was electric. Venetia wished she had the strength to run away, but her legs refused to move, and she was forced to remain where she was, looking at the man's inscrutable face and seeing the yellow cheeks faintly tinged with pink.

'You are certainly blunt,' he conceded at last. 'But we will not talk any more about the past. It is the present—and *your* behaviour—which interests me. Why did you decide to tell me your real identity?'

'I didn't want you to like me under false pretences. You are too nice to be fooled again, and also intelligent enough to accept that Margot was genuinely too ill to see you *tonight*.'

He was perceptive enough to catch her emphasis. 'You mean she will be better tomorrow?'

'Yes. That's why Neil didn't know what to do. If he'd told you Margot was ill tonight, and you found out that the next morning she was completely well again, you'd have wondered if he had lied to you.'

'You make it sound a most mysterious ailment if it can come and go so quickly.'

Without her being aware of it her eyes dropped to the glass of brandy he was holding.

'Ah,' he murmured, and gave a sigh. Then for the second time that evening he touched her arm. 'What is your real name?'

'Venetia.'

'It suits you better than Margot. I will not say anything to Neil about the deception. But you can tell him from me that I understand his problem, though I do not agree with the way he tried to solve it.'

'But you are not angry?'

'No. I would have been if I had discovered it for myself, but as *you* have told me—and also the reason for the pretence—I cannot be angry.' His glance was keen. 'You are tired. I can see that the evening has been a strain for you. We will go.'

'There's no need,' she protested, but he paid no attention. His eyebrows made an imperceptible movement, and as they rose, so did every Chinese in the room. Quietly but quickly goodbyes were made, though Lai-Kin was the last to leave.

'We will meet again,' he murmured to Venetia. 'I look forward to it.'

'No need to ask if you were a hit with Lai-Kin,' Neil said as they returned to the drawing room. 'You bowled him over.'

'Indeed I did,' Venetia replied nervously and, before she lost courage, said: 'I told him I wasn't Margot.'

'You did *what*?' It was an explosion of sound.

'I couldn't go on with the lie. He was too nice and—and—I was afraid he'd be furious if he found out the truth.'

'But he *wouldn't* have found out! That was the whole point of the exercise. Why on earth did you have to tell him?' Never had Neil been so angry. 'After all the trouble we went to ... when I *told* you the reason why I wanted you to pretend ...'

'It's because of that reason that I had to tell him the truth. And he wasn't angry—he was pleased.'

'Pleased!' he groaned.

'Yes,' she repeated. 'Pleased.'

Hurriedly she told him all that Lai-Kin had said, and as he listened, Neil's anger slowly disappeared, though he still looked shaken, and sat on the edge of a chair nervously drumming his fingertips on the small table beside him.

'You're right, of course,' he said as she came to the end of her story. 'There's no doubt he liked you—during our talk alone together he mentioned the fact—and had he ever discovered you *weren't* Margot ...' Neil's brows parted as his face cleared. 'The one major point that was blocking our trade talks has been finally solved. It's now only a matter of dotting the "i's" before we sign the Agreement.'

'That's wonderful. You must be feeling terribly pleased.'

'I'm pleased with *you*. It's obviously what you said to him during dinner that put him in the right frame of mind.'

The sharp peal of the telephone bell startled them both, and wondering who could be calling at such a late hour, Venetia hurried across to answer it.

It was Boris, his voice deep with amusement. 'Your visitors have gone, so I know I'm not interrupting you.'

'A good guess.'

'Not guesswork, darling. I saw them leave. I was in my car on the other side of the road.'

'Spying?' she asked coldly.

'What an outdated word! Let us say I was making sure of the ground before I covered it.' His voice went lower still. 'So you took over Margot's role tonight.' He heard her quick intake of breath and gave an unpleasant chuckle. 'If you employ servants, Venetia, you can never keep a secret. Neil should remember that for the future. Not that he'll have much of a future when this little story breaks.'

'Margot was too ill to come down. *You* saw to that.'

'So you stood in for her. A quick-witted action—I'll grant

you that—but it won't do any good. On the contrary, it will make things worse. Lai-Kin doesn't like being made a fool of, and when he learns what Neil did——'

'How will he find out?' she interrupted, curious to hear his answer.

'I've already taken steps to see that he's told.'

Here at last was justification for Neil's suspicions about Boris.

'I didn't know you were anti-British,' she said carefully.

'I feel nothing towards the British. It's the Chinese I'm concerned with. Like most Europeans, you underestimate them. Today they wish to be accepted by the world, but tomorrow they'll want to conquer it.'

'Perhaps if they're accepted in the right spirit——'

'Don't talk like a child!'

'Is *your* thinking adult?' she demanded.

'At least it's realistic. My country recognises what China's aims are, and we plan to stop them.'

'I thought you were stateless,' she retorted.

'I'm Russian.'

'Even though your parents had to run away?'

'They ran because they couldn't see beyond their own bank account!'

'And do you see so much further?'

Unexpectedly he chuckled. 'I enjoy talking to you, Venetia. It's a pity we cannot get to know each other better.'

'I don't think you'd ever get to know me, Boris. You've underestimated me all the way along.'

'Really?'

'Really,' she mocked. 'You see, I wanted to save you the bother of telling Lai-Kin the truth about my masquerade, so I told him myself.'

'I'm sure you did,' Boris said suavely. 'That's why you and Neil stood arm in arm by the door when he was leaving. It's a gallant lie, my dear, but not worthy of you.'

'It's the truth, Boris, though I don't expect you to believe me.'

'I don't.'

He hung up and for a second she stared blankly at the telephone before putting it down.

'I gather Kanin found out about our subterfuge,' Neil said.

'He doesn't believe I told Lai-Kin the truth.'

'Thank heavens you did!' Neil strode over and caught her shoulders. 'Do you know what this means? If Lai-Kin had learned the truth from Boris, I could have left Hong Kong here and now!'

'Perhaps you'll be more appreciative of a woman's intuition in the future!'

'I'll never discount yours,' he said, and before she could stop him he gathered her into his arms. 'I love you so much,' he said raggedly. 'I can't go on pretending any longer. I want to marry you.'

'No!' she cried, and pulled away from him. 'You love Margot.'

'I love *you*,' he repeated. 'I haven't loved Margot for years.'

'You've always acted as if you did.'

'That's all it was,' he said quietly. 'An act. My marriage was finished long before the accident. Margot knew it and begged me for a reconciliation. I told her it wouldn't work —that we should never have married in the first place—but the more I tried to make her see I didn't love her, the more she wanted me.'

'She can't bear being rejected,' Venetia said pityingly.

'She insisted we took a second honeymoon,' Neil continued as though he had not heard the interruption, 'and she deliberately got herself pregnant. She believed it was the one sure way of keeping me tied to her.'

'It probably was.'

'I wonder.' He shrugged. 'Anyway, it couldn't resurrect my love. It just made me feel guilty because I didn't! And then we had the car crash and my guilt exploded in my face. I blamed myself for everything. For the pregnancy, the accident, and finally her drinking ... everything. And I'd have gone on blaming myself if you hadn't come into my life.

Having you in my home—seeing you every day and talking to you, brought back my sanity; made me see that I couldn't go on sacrificing my life.' He caught her by the shoulders again. 'I love you and I don't intend to go on living in limbo. If Margot wants to destroy herself, then let her! But I won't let her destroy me as well.'

Venetia stared at him. She had known Neil was attracted to her, and wanted her, but never in her wildest dreams had she envisaged him saying he loved her and wanted to marry her.

'If you don't love Margot, why did you try and stop her from going away with Boris?'

He hesitated and then sighed. 'I considered it my duty to do so. I want to marry you—you've got to believe that—but I couldn't take my freedom without trying to stop Margot from ruining her life.'

'Then you'll never let her go!'

'I will. But I had to see if I could make her realise that she'll never be happy with Kanin. But she won't listen to me and I don't intend to stand in her way any more. If she wants him, she can go to him.'

Venetia shook her head. 'You'll never be free of her.'

'I'll always be worried about her,' he admitted, 'but I can't go on spoiling my life—or yours. We deserve a future together.'

'But you married her for love,' Venetia persisted. 'Are you sure it's all over?'

'My love was a dream,' he said bleakly. 'But when I woke up to it I was still bound to her by her dependency on me.'

'She's still dependent on you. If Boris lets her down she'll come back.'

'I won't be waiting for her. *You* are the woman in my life from now on. You and no one else.' He rested his cheek on hers. 'We were meant for each other, Venetia. I knew it the first time I saw you. Promise you'll wait for me till I'm free?'

'You know I will. But you'll never be free! Not if Margot needs you. I know you better than you know yourself.'

'You don't,' he said slowly. 'I've spent the last five agonising years trying to help her, and I cannot give her any more of my life.'

She longed to believe him but was afraid of doing so. 'You'll change your mind tomorrow, Neil.'

'Ask me in the morning and see.' He led her to the door. 'Come, darling, you must go to bed, you look exhausted.'

Together they went upstairs and he accompanied her along the corridor to her room. 'There's a lot to be said against chivalry,' he murmured, holding her close again. 'If I weren't a gentleman I'd force my way in.'

'You wouldn't need to use force,' she said tremulously.

His eyes darkened. 'Don't tempt me, darling, I'm only human.'

'I'll remember that for another night,' she whispered, and opening the door, slipped inside and closed it behind her before she could change her mind.

CHAPTER THIRTEEN

GOING into the dining room for an early breakfast, Venetia was disconcerted to find Neil already at the table. He looked as if he had slept as little as she had done, and seeing his glance at her own tired face, she knew he was thinking the same.

'I haven't changed my mind,' he said, even before she could say 'Good morning'. 'I still love you and I've every intention of getting my freedom.' He pushed back his chair and came over to her. 'What about you?'

'I'm going back to England.'

Shock registered on his face. 'You can't!'

'I can't do anything else. It's impossible for me to stay here now. You of all people should see that.'

'Then it will only be a temporary goodbye. My talks with the Chinese should be concluded within a month.'

'As soon as that?'

He nodded. 'Lai-Kin telephoned me this morning before returning to Peking. He reaffirmed our discussion last night—incidentally, he sent you his warmest regards—and has assured me we should be able to exchange documents before the month is out.'

'So you've got what you wanted?'

'For my country, yes. Now I intend to concentrate on my own affairs.' He caught her hand. 'You know what I feel about you. What more can I say?'

'Nothing more,' she said tremulously. 'If and when you are free, you will know where to find me.' She pulled her hand away from him. 'Don't talk about it again, Neil. I can't bear to think of a future that might never happen.'

'It *will* happen. I've already told you that.'

Gone was the detached, aloof man she had always known, and again he was impatient and passionate. Last night when he had averred his love for her, she had been afraid it had stemmed from unfulfilled desire and bitterness that Margot had let him down so badly, but this morning, with the success of his mission guaranteed and no reason for bitterness left, he still remained as vehement.

Sensing her thoughts, he said: 'When a dam is released it's impossible to stem the waters again; and you released the dam, my darling.'

The endearment trembled through her and she longed to throw herself into his arms and tell him she would wait forever, but thought of Margot prevented her. Poor, sick Margot.

'I still can't understand why you didn't get your freedom years ago,' she said bluntly. 'Last night you said you weren't happy with Margot even before the accident. Yet you stayed with her ...'

'She refused to give me a divorce,' he replied, 'and she knew I wouldn't deliberately create a scandal because of my career.' His sigh was audible. 'In those days my career was important to me, and by the time I realised how unimportant it was compared with personal happiness, it was too late to do anything.'

'Don't you feel it's too late now?'

'I'm thirty-seven,' he said bitterly. 'Is that too old to want love?'

'Oh no!' The words were forced from her, and with an effort she stopped herself from adding to them.

'It's best we don't talk about it any more,' he said into the silence. 'The next time I talk to you about the future, I hope I'll be free.' He pushed back his chair again and went to the door. 'About your return to England ...'

'I'm leaving this afternoon.'

'A woman of decision!'

'I'm playing safe.'

Across the distance of several yards they stared at each other, then with a lift of his shoulders Neil went out.

Venetia found it impossible to eat any breakfast. She heard Neil drive away and only then did she leave the dining-room. The maids were busy cleaning and she went to her bedroom and packed, wishing it were possible to leave the house without seeing Margot, but knowing she had to say goodbye and find some excuse for her sudden departure. She tried not to think of what Neil had said, and with her packing done she sat on the window seat and stared down at the view, wondering if she would ever see anything as beautiful again. But a future without Neil would never hold anything beautiful. Incredible to think that only a few months ago she had never known he existed. Even when she had first met him she had not been drawn to him. Yet indefinably he had woven himself into her life until now he was part of the very fabric of her existence.

To leave Hong Kong was the only solution. It was out of the question to go on living in the same house with him, partly because she knew neither of them would have the strength of mind to keep their relationship platonic if she did so, and partly because pity for Margot made her feel guilty.

Yet she was not to blame for Neil's change of heart. Neither by look nor word had she given him any encouragement. His love for her had occurred of its own volition.

But despite this knowledge, guilt was still with her as she went to Margot's bedroom. As she had expected, Margot was in bed, her lovely face showing no sign of the ravages of the night before. Only her expression—petulant and surly—gave any indication that she knew Venetia guessed why she had deliberately drunk herself into a stupor the previous evening.

'If you've come to tell me off——'

'I've come to say goodbye,' said Venetia. 'I'm returning to London.'

'Don't be silly!'

'I'm leaving this afternoon, I've already packed.'

Margot's mouth tightened. 'I suppose you're angry with me for letting Neil down?'

'There's no point in talking about it.'

'We *are* hoity-toity today!'

'Don't hurt him more than you have to,' Venetia blurted out, and stopped as she saw the smile that curved the wilful red mouth.

'How concerned you are about Neil. Anyone would think you were in love with him.' The smile grew wider still. 'I've noticed how you've always sided with him against me in the last few weeks. How you've always tried to put *me* in the wrong.'

'Most normal people *would*,' Venetia said bluntly.

'You think I'm bad for him, don't you? That you'd be better as a wife? Well, you'll get your chance soon enough. But you'll have to wait till I've gone to Boris. I'm not broadminded enough to let you take my husband while I'm still in the house!'

'Please stop it,' Venetia pleaded. 'You've no right to talk like this. Boris is wrong for you—he's wrong for *any* woman.'

'What gives you the right to judge him?' Margot replied savagely. 'Boris isn't a namby-pamby like Neil. He's——'

'He's cruel and domineering and he's used you,' Venetia said fearlessly. 'He deliberately encouraged you to get drunk yesterday because he——'

'Knew I wanted to hurt Neil!' The flaming hair glowed as the head tilted back defiantly. 'Don't blame Boris for what *I* did.'

'He hates England, too.'

Margot stared at her, then the anger left her face and she burst out laughing. 'So what! Do you think *I* care about England? Anyway, Boris doesn't really hate any country. Or love any country either, for that matter. He offers his services to any government who pays him.'

'You know that?' Venetia asked, astonished. 'Don't you care?'

'I only care about Boris.' Margot stood up, unmindful that she appeared almost naked in her transparent nightdress. 'If you're lucky, one day you'll love a man that way too. If it's Neil, I wish you joy of him!'

Venetia knew better than to reply. With Margot in this mood any retort would only make her more spiteful.

'If there's anything you would like me to do before I go——' she said expressionlessly.

'Nothing. If you're so keen to leave me, the quicker you go the better. You've gone back on your promise to stay with me till I leave Hong Kong.'

'I made that promise before I realised you were going to let Neil down—and your country too!'

'Go to hell!' Margot burst out.

Venetia left the bedroom, hurrying down the corridor before Margot had a chance to call her back. She had reached the top of the stairs when Margot's maid came running towards her, carrying a letter.

'Mr Kanin servant brought this,' she said. 'You please take to Mees Adams?'

Determined not to act as courier in this ugly affair, Venetia shook her head and continued on her way downstairs. She went into the library and carefully sorted through the small box file where she kept copies of all the correspondence she had dealt with since her arrival here. There was little enough to show for so many weeks' stay, and she could not help feeling that her time here had been a waste. Yet even as she thought this, she knew it was not true; her primary purpose—to encourage Margot to remain in Hong Kong until the trade talks were completed—had been successfully accomplished, though more from luck than judgment.

She had just closed the file when there was the sound of high heels racing down the stairs. Since all the servants wore slippers she knew it could only be Margot, and she went into the hall to see what was wrong. Margot was heading for the front door. Her face was ashen and her hair streamed wildly around her shoulders.

'What is it, Margot? What's happened?'

Without bothering to reply Margot ran down the steps and across the drive to where the car was parked. The chauffeur was not at the wheel and she wrenched open the door and slid into the driving seat.

Her expression was so wild that Venetia knew she could not let her drive alone, and she ran down the steps after her. 'Wait for me, I'm coming with you.'

'No, you're not,' Margot shouted. 'Get out of my way!'

The engine revved furiously and the car surged forward in a wild arc that made Venetia jump back so quickly that she fell against the steps, scraping the skin of her elbow. But she was too frightened by the look on Margot's face to be aware of any pain, and she jumped up and raced after the car, hoping to try and reach it as it stopped by the gate. But she was given no chance to do so, for it shot forward on to the road without a moment's hesitation, and with a squeal of tyres, roared down the hill.

Impelled by a frightening sense of urgency, Venetia ran back to the house; without knowing why she was desperately afraid. If only she could telephone Neil and ask him to go in search of Margot. Not that a search would be necessary; Margot was obviously on her way to Boris's flat, and it would be asking the impossible to expect Neil to go there to find her. Yet she could not forget the look of anguish on Margot's face, and she knew she would have no peace of mind unless she went after her herself. Unwilling to think what she could do when she found her, Venetia ran to collect her coat.

The door of Margot's bedroom was still open and automatically she glanced into it. A letter and an envelope lay on the carpet: the same envelope the maid had been carrying a few moments ago. Uncaring that she was prying, she stepped inside and picked it up. As she had expected, it was from Boris. But the contents came as a shock, and as the heavily scrawled words uncovered themselves in front of her eyes, she was appalled by the cruelty of them.

'By the time you get this I'll have left Hong Kong,' Boris wrote, the bold black letters echoing the life force of the man. 'You have served your purpose and there's no point pretending any more. I won't apologise for using you to try and destroy your husband's work because I know you were using me for the same reason. But it looks as if *he* has won for the moment. However, there will be other things I can do—perhaps not against him, but against others who think in the same innocent way. But I won't be needing your help, which causes me regret, of course, because you are an extremely desirable woman. Perhaps we will meet in the future. Till then, don't drink yourself to death.'

The signature 'Boris' came immediately afterwards. There was no word of love, nor even a 'sincerely', Venetia thought dully, though perhaps by not putting it Boris had been more sincere than he had ever been in his life.

She folded the letter and inserted it into the envelope. If Boris was leaving Hong Kong immediately then Margot must have gone to the airport to try and see him before he flew out. Not pausing to think any further than this, Venetia ran back down the stairs and into the kitchen.

The young servant who had driven her to Boris's flat the day before—was it only yesterday, she wondered fleetingly, it seemed to have happened aeons ago—was busy chopping vegetables at the sink, and at her shaky command he downed the wicked-looking knife he was holding and scurried outside.

His car was parked where he had left it yesterday. She climbed in and impatiently urged him to hurry.

'Same address as before?' he asked.

'Yes,' she replied, knowing even as she did so that it would be a waste of time.

As indeed it was, for Boris's servant told her his master had left for the airport an hour earlier. In the car again Venetia headed for the airport, ordering the boy to drive even faster. But though he grinned and sent the car rattling forward till it seemed they would almost take off from the road, he was forced to slow down at every bend, lest the inadequacy of their brakes sent them hurtling over the edge.

Down one hairpin bend after another they raced, but still she felt they were going too slowly. 'Can't you go any faster?' she begged.

Without looking at her, he shook his head, and from the way his shoulders were hunched over the wheel she knew he was forcing the engine to its maximum speed.

Another bend loomed ahead and they swerved round it. Brakes shrieked and the smell of rubber from burning tyres was acrid in her nostrils. She leaned forward nervously, fearful lest the engine might suddenly explode. The boy appeared to think so too, for he slowed down.

'Is it the tyres?' she asked.

'Not from our car,' he said, and pointed with one hand. Venetia followed his fingers with her eyes and with a jolt of fear saw that a gap had been torn in the railings bordering the side of the road. Two police cars were parked beside it and uniformed men were moving through the gap and out of sight.

'It is accident,' the Chinese told her. 'Is better if we drive more slowly.'

'Stop the car,' she ordered.

'Is not necessary to stop it completely,' he smiled.

'Stop it!' she said sharply, and was out of the seat and on to the road almost before he had done so. For the second time in twenty-four hours Venetia had a premonition. The first one had led to a successful conclusion, but this one was going to lead to disaster. She sped towards the broken rail and found her way barred by a policeman.

'You can't do anything,' he said.

'Was it a car?'

'Yes.'

'Where is it?'

'A long way down.'

'May I look?' Aware of his curious stare, she said: 'I'm not being ghoulish, but I—it's terribly important that I see what car it is.'

'A Daimler.'

The premonition was fast becoming fact, and her mouth went dry. 'Is it—was there a woman in the car?'

'How did you know?' He caught her arm. 'You saw the accident?'

'No.' The scene was beginning to swim around her, but she forced it to steady. 'I think I—I know who it is. Please let me look.'

Still holding her, he led her towards another policeman. He said a few quiet words to him, then guided Venetia over to the gap in the rail.

Fighting back her nausea, she peered down the incline. Fifty yards below, half hidden by bushes and boulders, the ruins of a smoking car could be glimpsed. Several policemen were around the wreckage and as she watched, one of them bent forward and dragged a figure free. It was too far away to see it clearly, but there was no mistaking the glint of red-gold hair. Venetia was glad for the hand under her arm, and she clung to it, shivering violently.

'You know her?'

She nodded, unable to speak, and the policeman drew her away from the side to one of the police cars.

The next few hours were a nightmare that ever afterwards remained hazy in her mind. She was aware of being questioned, of giving Margot's name and Neil's too, for suddenly he was there beside her, ordering her to be taken home to the house, and then taking command of the situation himself.

In her room she lay on the bed, not even bothering to take off her dress or shoes. Margot was dead. It was difficult to realise and impossible to accept. She and Neil had wanted him to be free, yet neither of them had guessed it would be obtained at the cost of Margot's life. Venetia buried her head in her hands and wept.

Again time passed. She must have fallen asleep, for when she awoke it was mid-afternoon. Changing into a fresh, pale green dress—she would not wear anything dark, for it smacked of hypocrisy to do so—she went down in search of Neil. She did not have to look for him, for he must have been listening for her step and came to meet her as soon as she reached the hall.

'How did it——?' she began.

'She was driving too fast and skidded,' he said, guessing her question. 'She lost control of the car and went over the side.'

'Do you think it was deliberate?'

'No.' Neil led her into the drawing room. 'She was trying to get to the airport to stop Boris.'

'Who told you?' Venetia couldn't hide her surprise that he knew.

'I found his letter in her room.'

'I see.' Legs shaking, she sat down. 'He killed her, you know. He couldn't have done it more deliberately if he'd murdered her.'

Neil walked over to the window and stared through it. He was wearing a dark suit and a black tie. It made him look paler and more withdrawn, and Venetia was reminded of the first time she had seen him. Her palms grew damp and she rubbed one against the other. Was conscience playing havoc with him too? Yet neither of them had cause for guilt. They had not taken their happiness at Margot's expense. Indeed they had decided not to take it at all until she had gone away with Boris and Neil was free.

A Sèvres clock on the mantelshelf chimed the hour, and looking at it Venetia knew she barely had time to get to the airport. 'I must catch my plane, Neil, or do you wish me to remain here?'

'Margot's body will be flown home,' he said quietly. 'I've already spoken to my father-in-law in London. She will be buried beside her brother.'

Venetia's eyes filled with tears. It was ironic that both brother and sister should have died by accident, and with all her heart she wished she could believe that Margot had found the peace she had been seeking for the last five years.

'The chauffeur will take you to the airport,' Neil continued. 'I hope you'll forgive me if I don't come to see you off?'

'I never expected it.' She held out her hand. 'I'll say goodbye now.'

He did not take her hand, nor did he come towards her, but remained by the window, a tall thin figure, remote and aloof with his grief. 'Goodbye, Venetia.'

'Goodbye, Neil,' she said, and walked out in silence.

In his usual mysterious way Sir William Blunden learned of Venetia's return, and a limousine was waiting when she stepped off the plane at Heathrow, to whisk her down to Wiltshire and her mother's cottage. The irritation she had felt towards her godfather during her stay in Hong Kong evaporated at this display of kindness. But then he always did the unexpected, and had an adroit ability to put himself in the right no matter how deeply he was in the wrong. Not that he had been wrong, she conceded, as the car wended its way down the narrow lanes, already leafy-green with early summer. He could not have guessed she would fall in love with Neil. He had chosen her to do a job and as far as he was concerned the job had been done. Margot's death was a tragedy no one could have foreseen.

It was a thought which Venetia repeated to herself many times in the days that followed, and reliving everything that had happened during her stay in Hong Kong, she knew that nothing she or Neil had done had precipitated it. Even Boris did not appear as black as she had first thought, for had he not come into Margot's life she would have found someone else to act as her nemesis. She had been doomed to tragedy; such high spirits and wilful temperament had forged its own destruction. The pity was that it had destroyed so much else on the way.

Surprisingly enough Venetia managed not to think of Neil, except on rare occasions when his narrow face would appear before her, disappearing again as she tried to see it more clearly. She wondered whether she was subconsciously trying to erase him from her memory, and as the days melted into weeks she knew she would have to, for she could not live her life in limbo, the way he had been content to do for so many years.

'I'm going back to London,' she announced to her mother that night.

'Can't you stay a bit longer? You still look frightfully pale.'

'I've been here a month and I've used up all my leave.'

'I'm sure William can get it extended for you.'

'No, darling,' Venetia said firmly. 'I need work to occupy me.'

Her mother contemplated the bowl of stocks she was arranging. 'You never did tell me the whole story of what happened in Hong Kong.'

'There wasn't much to tell. It all ended happily—from the Government's point of view.'

'I wasn't thinking about the Government. I mean Mr and Mrs Adams. Will he return to Hong Kong, do you know, or is his work completely finished there?'

'I don't know,' Venetia shrugged. 'It's not my concern any more.'

Saying the words aloud gave them a reality they had not had when she had said them to herself. Neil's silence in the past month had clarified the cold way he had said goodbye to her. If he used his logic he would know that his love for her had not caused Margot's death. Yet a guilt feeling—no matter how unjustified it was—could play havoc with one's intelligence, and he might well be holding himself responsible for the tragedy. How long he would continue to think this way she did not know. All she knew was that she could not remain here pining for him and waiting for him to see reason. Indeed he might never do so and that meant she must occupy herself with work and resume her social life. She would never forget Neil, but there would surely come a time when she would be able to think of him without wanting to weep.

'I'll go for a short walk in the woods,' she said aloud, and not bothering with a coat, left the house.

The countryside at this time of the year was particularly lovely. The air was warm yet not too dry, the earth still moist and crumbly. The fields around her were a carpet of variegated greens and golds, and she wended her way along a narrow footpath to reach the shade of the forest. Here the ground was far damper underfoot, and the bright sunlight was filtered by leafy boughs that rustled as an occasional bird flew out of the foliage. She had a favourite resting place on a fallen log, but she felt too nervous to sit down for long, and after a couple of moments she continued to walk again. An insect droned ahead of her, its wings reflected in a sunbeam, so that it seemed to be shot with silver and gold, as iridescent as a pearl. It reminded her of the gleaming satin dress she had worn the night of the dinner party when she had pretended to be Neil's wife.

Neil's wife. How far away that possibility was now! The memory of it was overwhelmingly painful, and the numbness that had enveloped her from the moment she had peered down the boulder-strewn incline to see the smoking black car broke like the cracking of melting ice, and resting against the trunk of a tree, she burst into a storm of tears.

She did not know how long she cried, except that her handkerchief was sodden, when some sixth sense told her she was not alone, and hurriedly wiping her eyes she turned round. Neil was standing a few yards away from her. In grey slacks and a darker grey sweater, he looked far different from the way she had last seen him. But it was more than a difference of clothes. In other ways he was different too. There was a square set to his shoulders and a firmer tilt to his head; or perhaps a burden had been lifted from him.

'What are you doing here?' she asked uncertainly.

'Do you need to ask?'

His voice was whimsical, but instead of being pleased by it she was annoyed. She had not heard a word from him for four weeks and now here he was, standing calmly in front of her as though they had only said goodbye yesterday.

'I'm going back to London tomorrow,' she said coolly. 'You could have saved yourself a journey.'

'I had to see you. Now. This minute.'

She shrugged. 'Another day wouldn't have mattered.'

'An hour longer would have been insupportable!'

She leaned against the bark of the tree, hoping its firmness would give her strength. 'Why?' she asked.

'For heaven's sake!' he burst out, and strode over to her. 'Have you forgotten what I said to you in Hong Kong? Doesn't it mean anything to you?'

Still she refused to meet his eyes. 'I wasn't sure what it meant to *you*. All these weeks ... no word from you ...'

'I had to let Margot rest in peace,' he said quietly. 'Until that happened I couldn't come to you freely.'

'And you are free now?'

'Not free of you, Venetia.'

She caught her breath and looked at him. He was smilling slightly, though he made no move to touch her. 'I don't want to—to trap you, Neil.'

'I've never met a more reluctant temptress! You've got no idea how much you mean to me, have you?'

'You've never shown me.'

'Lack of opportunity, my darling, not lack of desire! But I have the rest of my life—if you're willing to share it with me.'

'I couldn't bear not to,' she said on a sob, and flung herself into his arms. 'This last month has been agony. I thought you'd stopped loving me; that you blamed me for Margot's death.'

'No one is to blame for that.' He stroked Venetia's hair with a trembling hand and then his fingers rested on the nape of her neck. 'She was her own enemy and she paid the price for it.'

'It was such a wasted life.' Venetia was still tearful.

'All the more reason for us not to waste *our* life,' he said, and lifted her chin so that their eyes could meet. 'I know you thought I was heartless the way I let you leave Hong Kong, but I couldn't say anything to you then. Margot's death was still too close and——'

'I thought you didn't love me any more,' she repeated.

'I'll stop loving you when I stop breathing!' She smiled, and seeing her mouth curve, Neil touched it with his lips. 'I'll try not to make you cry again, Venetia. There'll be no more tears.'

'Don't say that.' She twined her arms around his neck. 'I always cry at weddings!' She pressed against him. 'I assume you *are* proposing?'

'You haven't a hope of getting away from me,' he said fiercely, and pulled her closer still. 'There's so much wasted time to make up for. Don't make me wait too long.'

'Whenever you want me,' she began, and had no chance to say more, for his mouth—hard and demanding on her own—told her it could not be soon enough for him.

Doctor Nurse Romances

Romance in the wide world of medicine

Amongst the intense emotional pressures of modern medical life, doctors and nurses often find romance. Read about their lives and loves in the four fascinating Doctor Nurse romances, available this month.

SURGEON'S CHOICE
Hazel Fisher

NURSE AT TWIN VALLEYS
Lilian Darcy

DOCTOR'S DIAGNOSIS
Grace Read

THE END OF THE RAINBOW
Betty Neels

Mills & Boon
the rose of romance

Best Seller Romances

Romances you have loved

Mills & Boon Best Seller Romances are the love stories that have proved particularly popular with our readers. They really are "back by popular demand." These are the other titles to look out for this month.

BRIDE AT WHANGATAPU
by Robyn Donald

'I want my son more than I want you,' Logan Sutherland told Fiona, but he was prepared to marry her — five years after the cruel rejection that had hurt her so deeply. He was arrogantly sure that he could make her love him all over again, just as a bonus — but Fiona meant to fight!

THE DARK SIDE OF MARRIAGE
by Margery Hilton

It was two years since the marriage of Nick and Karen Radcliffe had ended in disaster — but Nick's beloved adoptive mother didn't know that, and now that she was dying and wanted them near her, he was determined that she should not find out. And so Karen found herself forced once again to live with this man who had nothing but contempt for her — and trying desperately to control the longing she still felt for him...

ROOTED IN DISHONOUR
by Anne Mather

Beth was genuinely fond of Willard Petrie, which was why she had agreed to marry him and go to live in his Caribbean island home. But 'genuinely fond' was hardly the way to describe how she had begun to feel about Raoul Valerian. Could she fight the feeling and remain loyal to Willard?

Mills & Boon
the rose of romance

Best Seller Romances

Next month's best loved romances

Mills & Boon Best Seller Romances are the love stories that have proved particularly popular with our readers. These are the titles to look out for next month.

THE WILLING HEART
Helen Bianchin

THE MASTER FIDDLER
Janet Dailey

DISTURBING STRANGER
Charlotte Lamb

RING OF FIRE
Margaret Way

Buy them from your usual paperback stockist, or write to: Mills & Boon Reader Service, P O Box 236, Thornton Rd, Croydon, Surrey CR9 3RU, England. Readers in South Africa write to: Mills & Boon Reader Service of Southern Africa, Private Bag X3010, Randburg, 2125.

Mills & Boon
the rose of romance

4 BOOKS FREE
Enjoy a Wonderful World of Romance...

Passionate and intriguing, sensual and exciting. A top quality selection of four Mills & Boon titles written by leading authors of Romantic fiction can be delivered direct to your door absolutely FREE!

Try these Four Free books as your introduction to Mills & Boon Reader Service. You can be among the thousands of women who enjoy six brand new Romances every month PLUS a whole range of special benefits.

- Personal membership card.
- Free monthly newsletter packed with recipes, competitions, exclusive book offers and a monthly guide to the stars.
- Plus extra bargain offers and big cash savings.

There is no commitment whatsoever, no hidden extra charges and your first parcel of four books is absolutely FREE!

Why not send for more details now? Simply complete and send the coupon to MILLS & BOON READER SERVICE, P.O. BOX 236, THORNTON ROAD, CROYDON, SURREY, CR9 3RU, ENGLAND. OR why not telephone us on 01-684 2141 and we will send you details about the Mills & Boon Reader Service Subscription Scheme — you'll soon be able to join us in a wonderful world of Romance.

Please note:— **READERS IN SOUTH AFRICA** write to Mills & Boon Ltd., Postbag X3010, Randburg 2125, S. Africa.

Please send me details of the Mills & Boon Reader Service Subscription Scheme.

NAME (Mrs/Miss) _____ EP6

ADDRESS _____

_____

COUNTY/COUNTRY _____

POSTCODE _____

BLOCK LETTERS PLEASE